A DOMAIN OF HER OWN

AN ANTHOLOGY
OF ART, POETRY, AND PROSE
BY MEMBERS OF THE NLAPW
CENTRAL NEW YORK BRANCH
CELEBRATING OUR 100TH YEAR

Edited by
Nancy Avery Dafoe
and
Susan Wolstenholme

PEN WOMEN PRESS

For book information, contact dafoe.nancy@gmail.com

Cover design: Lucy Arnold
Book Editor Coordinator: Lucy Arnold

ISBN: 978-1-950251-21-6

First edition
Printed in the United States of America

BISAC codes: POE001000 POETRY/Anthologies;
ART065000 ART/Women Artists; LC0019000
LITERARY COLLECTIONS/ Women Authors

This is a collection of poetry, prose, and art; incidents are
the product of the authors' imaginations or are used
fictitiously. Any resemblance to actual persons, living or
dead, is coincidental.

Published in the United States by
the National League of American Pen Women, Inc.
PEN WOMEN PRESS (PWP)

Founded in 1897, The National League of American Pen
Women, Inc. is a nonprofit dedicated to promoting the
arts. NLAPW, Inc., 1300 17th Street, NW, Washington,
D.C. 20036-1973
www.nlapw.org

DEDICATION

In our 100th anniversary year of the Central
New York (CNY) Branch of the NLAPW, we
dedicate this collection to visual artists,
writers in every genre, composers, musicians,
dancers, designers, and all women who
engage in the arts, who support and
encourage one another in promoting
the arts in our communities
and in our lives.

Sally Stormon, art

ALSO, BY
THE CNY BRANCH
OF THE NLAPW

In the Company of Women,
An Anthology Commemorating the
90th Anniversary of the CNY Branch of the
NLAPW

Edited by Lorraine Arsenault and
Nancy Avery Dafoe
MLMG Designs, © 2016

Art Speaks, The Catalogue

Edited by Nancy Avery Dafoe
Published by PEN WOMEN PRESS, 2021

Correspondence to
dafoe.nancy@gmail.com

Contents

Titles may be abbreviated in TOC

**Celebrating 100 years of the
CNY Branch of the NLAPW**

After Coffee and Crossants with Therese

I can only imagine her den, her studio,
her hoard of stuff –
     paints, pens, tools, and glues,
     fabrics and papers of every size and shape,
     pieces in progress and pieces set aside—
a veritable artistic dig, a trove
autobiographical and archeological,
a place where inspiration is crafted
and recrafted into stunning creations.

I can imagine, too, as in taking pen to paper,
how a lifetime of story and inspiration
     stored in albums and files,
     diary notes and faded drafts
can return to mind, be reconsidered
and take on new dimensions,
rustle memory to life again,
become material for a new telling,
a new collection,
here, between these covers.

Mary L. Gardner

Susan Carmen, art
"The Stars are Best Seen at Night"

Made in New York exhibition at the
Schweinfurth Art Center
(Used with permission)

I dreamed sailboats

"Bury me at sea," said my forty-something father.
His own father died at 53 so he figured
it was time to plan his own funeral.

We were sailing, just the two of us.
The wind had died
but the relentless current of the river pushed
the boat along.
During the summers of my childhood,
and my teenage years,
my father and I went sailing every morning,
him at the helm of the boat he'd built himself.
"When I die," Dad told me, "set my boat on fire,
"Put my body in first, and let it sink
in the river at sunset."

Teenage me thought that was cool.
The Saint Lawrence is a big river, wide and deep,
and on summer nights, the sun paints the sky
red and purple above the Canadian shore.

Perhaps my 94-year-old father has forgotten
that conversation we had fifty years ago.
But last night, I dreamed a parade of sailboats,
a procession of sailboats, a spectacular line
of sailboats, gliding down a red river
below a purple sky. With stars so bright

they made the night sky ripple.
The sailboats carried casks of red wine
and musicians blowing into trumpets.
My father's body burned as his sailboat
swept past little towns and tall grey cliffs
leaving a trail of smoke and jazz,
a warrior going towards eternal feasting and battle.

In my sixties, I know things that
teenage me did not.
I could not have predicted
my oldest sister would die first, or my mother
would disappear into dementia,
or that I would be the one
entrusted to plan my father's journey
towards the halls of Valhalla.

Janine DeBaise

Let Morning Come

after Jane Kenyon's "Let Evening Come"

Let the darkness of the long night
recede from the city's rooftops, blending
morning with mourning as the sun rises.

Let the taxis barrel down the streets
as if there were somewhere to go beyond
this hospital room. Let morning come.

Let the unopened envelopes pile up
in the mailbox. Let sunlight pour into
your kitchen where dishes still litter the sink.

Let pictures in their frames recall happier days.
Let the neighbors wonder about the woman
taken away in an ambulance. Let mourning come.

To the milk carton in the refrigerator, to the blinking
light on the answering machine, to the ones
left behind, let morning come.

Let cold wind blow, as it will, and don't
be afraid. Grief is the outer fabric of a coat
lined with gratitude, so let mourning come.

Gloria Heffernan

Field Notes: Hand

Subject studied
in natural habitat:

It chops the onions
for tonight's chili.
Observe the way the fingers
curl around the knife handle
making smooth vertical cuts
that release the gases
that burn the eyes
and summon the tears.

Watch it clip the leash
to the dog's collar,
and coil the long strap
twice around the wrist
to keep a firm hold
in case he decides to chase
the neighbor's cat.

Study the way it handles
the steering wheel,
the subtle movements
that keep the car centered in the lane,
the easy flick of the index finger
turning the blinker on,
the smooth return to the wheel.

Observe it like a scientist
on a field expedition studying
the behavior of a moth—
so common a thing
until you try to count its wingbeats
or describe its flight pattern.

And then a meat cleaver
falls from the sky

Gloria Heffernan

What Saves Me

for the woman riding her bike
down Cascadilla Street

The click of pedals
and sweat on my right knee
as it rises and falls
rises and falls
in turn with the left one –
that will save me.

The dappled sunlight
through these neighborhood trees
kiss my cheeks furtively
who can resist?
July brings her passion –
that will save me.

This blue yoga mat
rides along merrily
strapped onto the crossbar
bouncing with glee
to class and its stretching -
That will save me.

In love with freedom
I lean back, pop a wheelie

and connecting with clouds
I laugh out loud
find my Yes! in this world
Yes. That will save me.

Stacey Murphy

Susan Murphy, art

When the Winds Shift

*After "Self Portrait as a Farmer's Daughter" by Sam
Rathbun*

I chop wood at dusk
and await the fireflies
Sweat beading at the back of
my knees and above
my top lip
And
I know what to do if an
early skunk shuffles past in the grass
And
I know what to do if a
snake crawls from the rockpile
And
I even know what to do if a
black bear waddles out of the woods

But
instead of a skunk or a snake or a black bear
it is this man
who says he was camping but is lost
And
I ask how long
And
he says five days but
he does not smell like five nights of woods

I know because the wind shifts as he steps closer
And
I keep my axe poised because
skunks, snakes, and even black bears
can usually be ignored or respected

But
I learned too young that
a lying man with a sweaty grin
is not something to
take my eye away from

Stacey Murphy

Rescue at Koko Crater

He descended like a spider from a slender thread.
The chopper blades whirred above the trail.
"Don't be afraid," said his partner.
From the top of the volcano, I could see
a crowd in the parking lot below.

"Don't be afraid," they said,
snapping me into a canvas harness,
"He's the best in the business," said one firefighter.
"I'd let him carry my mother," said his partner.

He hooked my harness to his belt with a steel
carabiner. "Don't be afraid," he said. "We lift cars
with these things." If I could have moved the muscles
of my face, I might have smiled.

He signaled the pilot and we rose in sudden whoosh,
dust and stones swirling in the vortex.
His body was taut as the cable that carried us.
"Don't be afraid," he said.
"Thirty seconds and we'll be back on the ground."

We glided over the turquoise face of Hanauma Bay,
its half-moon coastline fringed with palm trees.
"You might as well open your eyes," he said.
"Tourists can't buy a view like this."
So, I looked, and I wasn't afraid.
Gloria Heffernan

Sailing

A dead roach floats on the surface
of my mother's afternoon coffee.
She watches its compatriots
scale the wall above the stove
as if they know she cannot
douse them with Raid
while dinner is cooking.
She doesn't know if roaches laugh,
but she imagines they do on days like this
when all the scrubbing in the world

seems to be for naught.
She dumps the coffee down the drain
and wipes her hands
on the green housecoat she wears
to hang out the window
clipping freshly laundered sheets to the clothesline,
watching them snap and billow in the wind
like the graceful sails of a schooner
she wishes she could board with her children
and sail away to someplace clean.

Gloria Heffernan

Marilyn Forth, art

For a Day I Wanted to Be Amy Tan,
sketching a dark-eyed Junco in my yard
as carefully, as perfectly as she,
making bird chronicles the only ambition
of my sorrowing.

Moving charcoals across silent white papers
in which sadness is stilled
in this investment in bird feather and call,
    I listen, not casually but well.

When I heard repeated, urgent notes of a robin
                    perched on a branch
touching my window,
    his mate far too preoccupied
    with little blue eggs in their nest.

And I am overwhelmed with the movement of
slowing
until I hear
all the way down
    to another time, another country where
            I trekked carefully through Costa Rican
            jungle with my grandsons and young
            guide, our footfalls nearly silent as we
            struggled
in the lush, dense heat of our nighttime journey—

where the weight of aging and loss
            is suddenly diverted to
a procession   of   leaf-cutter   ants—
near our feet, ants carrying
far more
than their own weight,
keeping the path
free and undisturbed.

Nancy Avery Dafoe

Phantom Corals, A Warning

Winter in summer.
Water creatures drowning in their water world.
This paradox
silent suffocating—these living entities
struck ghost-like
as pigment drains away.

Pigments once as colorful as rainbows
under the sea: greens, pinks, yellows, reds, purples,
and blues
d   i   s   a   p   p   e   a   r   i   n   g—
corals becoming ivory bone—
skeleton sculptures until
final decay.

A too rapidly warming planet
altered by man's indifference,
annihilating greed, waste, and carelessness
will extinguish these hydroid creatures
dwelling in our tropical seas,
these tiny organisms
that have been highly successful and around
since the last days of the dinosaurs.

Once more biodiverse than rainforests,
coral reefs now assaulted, maimed by overfishing,
our oily sunscreens, and our insatiable appetite for

all things PLASTIC.

Ocean temps rising as a result of our demands
for oil extracted from the sea bed,
our gluttony, our factory farms
and increasing CO2 production,
our industries and wastes bathing the waters.

And when the corals go—
when their ecosystems fail,
these miraculous life-sustaining coral reefs
made up of tiny animal bodies of polyps—
so goes marine life—some 830,000 species of it,
one quarter of all ocean organisms
dependent on the reefs—
so goes ecotourism and the almighty dollar,
billions worldwide.

To say nothing of the fact that these reefs
protect our coastlines, our shorelines
from more rapid erosion,
limiting coastal destructive wave energy
or, to put it bluntly,
reefs stave off shoreline eradication.

That should get your attention.
WARNING. WARNING. WARNING!

But back up.
Above the surface of the seas, pelicans and osprey
shadows are seen patrolling, sunlight glinting
off waves like reverse constellations.

Start again with vision.
Enter the way you enter the ocean:
diving in with a metaphoric splash,
feeling your way around
as you slowly come to know what at first
seemed alien.

You begin to recognize coral reef lines
in this space in which you are the stranger,
that foreign intruder.

Immersed in water like dreaming—
sights fantastical

but, perhaps, fatal. Maybe, if we made death
visible through art, people would stop,
take notice, and think.

Coral in nearly infinite variety.
Digitate corals like stubby fingers raised.
The brain coral immediately determined
for its uncanny resemblance to the human brain
even though the creature
is composed of tiny polyps.

Mushroom corals resemble multiplying starfish.
Leaf corals remind us of an animate
head of lettuce,
and elkhorn corals branch out
like the horns on an elk, of course.
Sea pen corals make us think of feathers
or feather pens, and Gorgonian corals
suggest intricate connections
of a tree and multitude of branches growing outward.

Boulder star, great star,
mustard hill,
slimy sea plume,
and fire coral forming
over thousands of years—
now dying off in a few.

These creatures that resemble plants
reach beyond their limitations of size and mobility
through ingenious means. They call the algae
to them, but the algae are leaving, choked out.
These spectacular 6,000 species of anthozoans,
these organisms in the phylum Cnidaria,
these corals host symbiotic algae.
And one with clown fish, too.

Then you swim up and out for air,
lean in to learn nearly all plastics made
have not been recycled but dumped,
breaking down into particles that never leave,
leaching chemicals in their disastrous wake.

Plastics that inhibit cyanobacteria growth,
block sunlight, these floating rafts of pathogens.
Eleven billion pieces of plastic in our oceans.

Plastic microparticles fouling our waters:
bags—sandwich and grocery bags,
Ziploc bags, water bottles, bandages,
bins, bumpers, buckets,
body wash in bottles, bottles for water,
bottles for medicines, boots,
combs, cups and cup lids, clothes, cases,
cosmetics, grocery carts,
coffee pods, cutlery,
CD cases and CDs, contact lens,

cigarette filters, carpeting, cooking timer,
wall coatings, and car parts;
dental floss,
extrusion coating, envelopes,
fishing nets and lines,
food containers, furniture, frames,
face masks, fabrics,
fireworks, coffee filters,
glitter, gum,
lamination products, light bulbs,
metal lids with inner coating of plastic,
nail polish, nylon, non-stick pans,
pill containers, paper plates,
polypropylene chairs,
pumps for inhalers,
and other kinds of pumps;

plastic wrap, produce stickers,
package cushioning,
make their insidious way
through to suffocating
corals,
marine life,
endangering all ocean life.

Corals ingesting microplastics
Corals, like mine canaries of the sea,
ominously fading away.

Where is the language of such loss?
Unending winter in summer?
Toward loss of even vowels and consonants
that once fell so easily from our tongues.

Even silence struck dumb.
Until absence is all, after all.

Nancy Avery Dafoe

Darlene Yeager-Torre, art
Central Ohio Branch NLAPW
(Used with artist's permission)

memories in seasons

across the lake
Highland Forest beckons,
yellows, green and burnt orange,
clustered together,
small houses
dotted ups and downs,
and Canadian geese making their way
across the blue-grey water.

a slight chill in the air
of what is to come,
and the green still sits on the hills
before frost and winter's cold,
makes its mark
of white stillness
ice and snow.

four feet of snow,
lurking
making simple walking or driving
treacherous,
holding my breath,
till my footing
went forward
for a new beginning,

as sunlight peered
through the frozen
sky and warmed
the time with hope.

Nancy Keats Benson

Marilyn Forth, art

Sharon Souva, fabric art,
"Geomorphology"
(turned for larger size)

A Flight of Swallows Flew Through

When birds return from their 4,000-mile journey,
swallows seem to signal hope and renewal,
as if we had been waiting for them before waking
to our senses dulled by Winter's cold.

Like poets' promising flights of fancy
in morning air awash with light,
angels and angles of birds flying in dazzling
space through time in bursts of energy,

this image could be a page out of poet's journal,
with metaphors inherently artful,
yet an honest attempt to offer layers
of meaning in tenor carried by these vehicles in
flight.

Barn swallow not really like the poet
except in agility; the poet with words, perhaps,
likened to swallows' fantastic aerial patterns
making meaning in momentum.

This flight of swallows flew through me
with a flutter of wings tickling;
their tiny sharp beaks making a thousand
infinitesimal slices of life on the wing;

swallows with their long, forked tails
leaving wisps that could be followed like the wakes
from small boats on calm lakes; these tiny birds
with their reddish-brown throats and peachy-white
colored chests, all contrast under sun glint off
blue-black masked heads now blur of movement
in moment. Their wings in artful, sharp curve—
mathematical; birds capturing light.

These expert aviators leave life-trails
we may follow in their wake,
out of our long sorrowing
where the dead still sleep.

Nancy Avery Dafoe

Heed The Call

Your truest place waits in the hush of twilight's
breath.
Shadows reach and whisper secrets,
A voice not loud, but relevant and clear,
Calls your name for you to hear.

Step gently through the silver seam,
Beyond the many veils you have crossed,
A holy trail awaits.

When broken bones sprout feathered wings,
When ashes curl in sacred flame,
Not death, but change.

The shedding skin,
The place where all new things begin.

You are the storm, and still you rise,
Like the sun rebelling against the midnight skies.

This is not the fall nor the end,
This is your soul.
Heed the call.

Nicole Marie Mastropool

Wild Woman

We are filled with a yearning for the wild,
a fire that burns deep within,
though we are taught to feel shame for such desires.
We carry that longing with us,
but society shrouds it in guilt,
teaching us to suppress what calls to us.
We used to hide our passion beneath long hair,
but the wild woman within never left.
She persists through the days and nights.

No matter where we are,
the soaring shadow follows us,
a beast that will never be tamed.
Overcast,
it feels like a storm lurking in our light,
but we seek only the truth.
Never mind the worm.
It's the wild that calls, and we listen.
Even the most confined woman clings to her wild
nature.
She knows deep down, instinctively, that one day,
an opportunity will arise.

A chance to escape,
she will run wild and free.

Nicole Marie Mastropool

Lawless

Mother Nature outlives us.
Her brilliance shines even in the most battled lands.

She is lawless.

Here we sit with our tools and things,
Taking up her space as if it's ours to keep.

Our laws are spread about the barren soil,
We forget all Earth's spoils.

Running about in our day-to-day lives,
Evil v. Evil
The light hides in obvious shapeshifter forms.

A vicious circle of life and death,
But even with all of our rules,

The reality is,
We are lawless.

Nicole Marie Mastropool

Vanessa Johnson, art
"Last Tree"

The Last Tree

The last tree lifted its branches into the heavens and cried out unto the Mother of all creation, "I am lonely."

There was no one left living on the Earth except the last tree. Not one man nor beast, not one plant nor insect. Not one living thing. No life was left to hear the last tree's anguished cry in the barren forest that used to be its home.

Dark jaundiced clouds hung low and deadly. Heavy unrelenting heat scorched the red sky. Pounding winds twisted the tree's ancient trunk and branches. Not a drop of water existed to offer merciful relief. The tree's once beautiful and lush leaves were forever gone. It could not regenerate, could not grow anymore. The tree's brittle voice cracked and moaned echoing centuries of sorrow. "I am lonely.

Man had ravished the Earth; polluted its waters, air, and lands. Killed every breathing thing. And in doing so...destroyed themselves. This last tree, this tree of life... and of death, was the last to bear witness to a dying planet.

The tree remembered providing shade for the living. Remembered being a part of the life cycle of water and its continual rebirth. It remembered breathing carbon dioxide and gifting the planet with oxygen. Of sacrificing limbs for drums, and cradles, and shelters for mankind and animals, and bees. Of rituals and circle dances at its feet celebrating births, and marriages, and deaths.

It remembered what man had forgotten. The dance of reciprocity and communion that those first born on earth once honored. Of care and not dominion. Of stewardship and not destruction.

The Mother creator threw open the heavens and opened her arms. She had heard the last trees' cries and tears fell from her eyes. Her fingers intertwined with the tree's tender twigs. Her breasts fed the tree's crumbling bark and her lips kissed the tree's last falling leaf. The Mother braided the tree's roots in her own hair. And in a shining bright cool light, the tree was lifted from the hell of man's creation to the golden heavens. The last tree was lonely no more.

Vanessa Johnson

Artwork collaboration by Vanessa Johnson
and Robin Tobias Kasowitz

Woman In The Window,
Remembering Rosa Parks

She lay in state, a woman of uncommon grace.
She defied historic caveat and chose honor, not place.

Famous now in windowed profile, she stared at
everything, at nothing, as though the bleak December

day could bring her strength, calm her beating heart,
take away fear, let the might of will dry any tear.

She must have known what lay ahead:
metal bracelets, a numbered photo, a narrow bed.

To all who heard that day, power spoke to power
and a mighty roar went up to claim that hour

for history, as wheels slowed and marching feet
in lock-step cadence stormed the streets.

Out of the long silence, ancient anthems rose
like armored battle cries turned on dreaded foes.

Slowly, a nation moved to meet the promise
of its founding dream and those who bore it final
witness.

She lay in state, coffined in a marble hall,
while footsteps fell in solemn lines, a requiem for all.

No simple woman, she of few words and abundant
hope, held a nation to account, her life beyond
camera's scope.

Mary L. Gardner

Vanessa Johnson, fabric art

Crush on a Dead Guy

Be a fool for love, for yourself, what you think might possibly make you happy, even for a little while, whatever the cost or consequence might be.
—Anthony Bourdain 1956 - 2018

Gonad. Right here, in the first line. Clinical. Not for
shock either. Tony would like it that way. He didn't
cotton to softening the blow with genteel sweetbread.
Just the base truth of nature. Just a pluck at the throat.

The sweet spot of love once deep inside me
is cauterized. Someone I never knew is dead
as well; handsome and driven. Tortured,
one might say. Familiar only with his fame,

I mourn his voice, his weathered face on the screen.
That's how it is sometimes; love beyond reach and
all. A late-show host, the one who has taken to plaid
cotton shirts with no tie, cashmere sweaters in muted
tones.

That guy. I fall asleep to his voice most nights,
the tv on a timer. Well, the other night before I woke
up, he was lying in bed next to me. A moment after
that, he walked to the window, unceremoniously
ending the affair.

So much cleaner to dream a man. Much less work.
Being found out, the only possible humiliation.

What a relief, waking up. I'm not even trying
to believe in trust. I've no further use for subtlety.

Georgia Popoff

Rachel Dickinson, art

a home with a soul

rich red
goldrush orange,
peaked roofs
and the one chair

someone is coming out
to sit
to think
to create

time is held still
as trees in the background
listen
for the house
to dream
to speak
to soar.

Nancy Keats Benson

Sally Stormon, art

Poem #3: Pandemic later days, early spring (2021)

Despite everything
Tiny snow drops
White through white
Peep their heads
To remind us what
Flowers look like
Just when we thought
we had forgotten.

And we
Not as brave
With great caution
Begin to step out
From our warm safe houses
Into a world of trouble
To remind ourselves that we
Are still alive.

Susan Wolstenholme

A Little Bird Told Her

"You don't need an invitation to sing," the bird insisted, exasperated.

"What if my song isn't good enough?" Olivia countered, already sticky from the morning heat.

"Birds never wonder if their song is worth singing. We never ask ourselves if we can sing like the nightingale."

"No bird would stop her!" Olivia breathed in, glaring defiantly. Out came the blues, not smooth or sultry, but the syncopation of a life lived true to her own unique cadence. The mangroves fell silent until the seagrass began to sway.

Following Olivia's lead, birds joined, softly at first, then bursting into soulful rhythm.

Birds of a Feather

"I'm such a fool," Olivia lamented, tears rolling
down her
cheeks.

"You're the smartest person I know," reassured the
bird. "And the bravest."

"What if I never find my place?" Olivia whispered,
confiding her greatest fear.

And the bird remembered how hard it is to be young.
She recalled desperately clinging to a mangrove tree,
a fledgling barely sheltered from the hurricane's

wrath. How small last night's thunderstorm seemed in comparison. And how joyful to sing on a clear blue-sky morning.

"Dear one," the bird encouraged. "All you need is faith to let go of control and trust the journey."

Art bird glass sculptures by Sheila M. Byrnes; Bird Stories by Gretchen Martens

Sally Stormon, art

Tea for All the Broken Places

Her porch so inviting
designed almost Gatsby-like,
whispers welcome.
Soft tones muted like our friendship,
drift toward the sidewalk.
Bright colors: orange, turquoise, yellow,
spell warmth.
They belie winter's approach.
We will soon be pummeled by snowstorms.
Subtle whimsy abounds.
Here a metal rooster, there
a round, green pitcher
brimming with blue hydrangea.
You wonder how you could have stayed away so
long?
Smiles mingle with conversation and forgiveness.
Finally broken no more you visit.
Years of yearning evaporate.
Her musings a balm.
Hot tea slips through your cracks.
She offers insight and hope.
Her husband's Parkinson's? Not a trouble,
only one more thing to cradle with love.
The toasted apple muffin she offers, so buttery and
warm, wraps your heart in richest pops of red.

Janet Fagal

After the exile

After the exile from paradise, Eve finds herself sneaking away to write letters to Snake. She pokes them into bottles to toss into the sea. Sings them into the air. Tucks them into crevasses, traces them into dust at the bottom of canyons – anywhere she can imagine her words might be borne to her friend, who she still believes meant no harm. And even if he didn't…well. He was hilarious and relatable, far more entertaining than Adam.

One day, some archaeologists might come across one of the bottles. Bottle #32, let's say, and if they open it, they will find this message:

"My dear serpent friend,
It has been a long time without your company and though I am supposed to be ashamed, and hate you, and fear you with a depth so deep that all my daughters will carry my fear in their own bones, I just don't feel these things. I cannot stop wondering at the last riddle you started to tell me while Adam was having his snack on that last day. That possibility of that last half-conversation fills my days with something more interesting than moving, hunting, finding water, moving again, and the constant search for something to wear.

"Adam is such a fearful man. He took the Almighty's
words WAY more harshly than I, won't even watch
me undress at night. I mean, he didn't notice I was
naked at all before, except when we touched, but now
he only notices for the sake of trying so hard to NOT
notice. God has let me know, dear friend, that I am in
the right on this matter. The shame is all something
Adam's taken on, his own construct, his own Hell.
I'd gladly give it up and prance around without my
fig leaves, again. The great I Am would be fine with
it, I know this - but even mentioning it upsets Adam
far too much. God is concerned that Adam's
insecurities have become far too strong to even feel
his light any longer, to even remember who or what
he is praying to each night.

"Oh, my slithering friend. I wish I could shed skins
and magically rejuvenate like you. At least hearing
the end of your last riddle would be a nice way to fill
an afternoon. So, if you ever get this and find a
way…I would love to hear from you.

Your pal, Eve"

Stacey Murphy

Summer 1980

Had I not left the brutally hot sublet off Mass Ave,
just a 7-minute walk to Harvard Square, I may have
grown accustomed to the kimchi and Korean BBQ
festering in the dumpster in the alley beyond my
bedroom window. I might have finally found a job, a
new apartment, a future in the city. If I hadn't left, I
would have learned the T lines to the suburbs,
perhaps become an urgent driver who typically rolls
through red lights, bought a second home on the
Cape. I may have become an ardent Red Sox fan. If I
had remained in Cambridge, I might have gotten a
part-time job at Grolier Poetry Book Shop and spent
most of my paychecks on first editions. If I had
stayed, I would have been so far from my father, but
then, if I had stayed, he might have not died after all.

> There are only choices,
> no answers. The universe
> conspires for our success.

Georgia Popoff

The Saint of Snow

In the habit of February,
this frosty day had no scent
until halfway up the drive
an unmistakable musk
stopped your shovel in mid-scrape
and you went still except your eyes that
scanned the frozen neighborhood.
No movement
stretches of white lawn unmarked
yet the sudden scent was strong -
skunk or fox -
no tracks, just a hole by the
pipe under the driveway,
and you imagined circles of fur
snug and resting,
the Saint of Snow sending
soft reminder of rejuvenation
to you too – let yourself recuperate,
prepare for meaningful action to come.

Stacey Murphy

Sweeping Ice

We walk to a nearby pond to skate wearing our rubber boots, as we don't have money for skates. My sister arrives first to sweep the snow off the ice. Her scream of "Help!" sends me running. She's fallen through, and the surrounding ice is treacherous, breaking as I try to reach her. The broom's still on the ice, and I remember a commercial where a person used an oar to rescue someone. I hand her the broom. Her hands slip on the slick handle. I shout, "Use your teeth!" As she bites, I slowly pull her from the water.

Sheila M. Byrnes

Sally Stormon, art

Vectors in Ink

Sometimes the mind sees things
the eye does not yet see.
When you wake in early morning,
before you kick off covers
and attempt to orient yourself,
you open your eyes and take in light
from windows and doorway.
Then you quickly close your eyes
against a streaming pool
of light—white setting-off black squares—
these apparitions appear
imprinted as if captured in negative
at the exact angle your head
is turned on the pillow.

If you close your eyes
and look into this imprint zone
for a while longer, you can see
distortions created by disappearing
light, and then you seem to examine
your own iris and pupil in reverse.
In the middle, tiny blue dots begin
to move outward from the center
where they were tightly congealed
into nearly solid mass.
(Continued on page 55)

**Stephen Carpenter, art
"Eye Sparkle—
Retinal Apparitions"**

Appearing at the *Made in New York* exhibition
at the Schweinfurth Art Center, Auburn, NY.

(Used with the artist's permission.)

There are something less
than ten million cones
on the retina of each eye
but more than ten times as many rods.

Millions upon millions of blue dots
speed away from the center,
opening up empty space,
and you now imagine
you are looking at the beginning
of the universe
in your mind's eye.

Nancy Avery Dafoe

Graduate Students on a Hot Tin Roof

The sheep, with their little colored bands around their bellies, had shaded up for the afternoon, while I sat on a hot tin roof in the mid-day sun recording their activity or lack thereof. I took a swig from the thermos Bruce handed me and adjusted the hat to shade my eyes.

"What do we have to eat?" Bruce asked, taking the thermos back from me.

I dug through the bag lunch I'd packed in the morning and handed him a sandwich. We'd been there since morning, getting up early, packing a lunch, driving five miles along the back road from campus to the summer pastures the university used for its flock of sheep. We'd let the sheep out of the shed whose roof we were sitting on into the five-acre pasture where they'd graze all day. Meanwhile, we were recording their grazing behavior. What quadrant they grazed in, how long, who with. The pasture was divided off into sections, each marked with colored flags, so we could note the color of the section of pasture, and the color of the band around the sheep and map out a day of grazing.

On the south and eastern edges of the pasture were woods and so in the heat of the day, the sheep would gather together in the shade of the trees and lay chewing their cud. We, the graduate students recording their movements, sat on a tin roof in the blazing sun watching them. Bruce, having finished his sandwich, lay back on the blanket we were sitting on and pulled his cap over his face. I dug a paperback out of my backpack.

"Wake me up when they start to move," he said.

I took another drink, opened the book, and settled down to read. We'd been in Corvallis, Oregon for 2 years by then, both working on Masters Degrees in Animal Science studying sheep behavior or genetics. I'd already heard plenty of people willing to tell me how stupid sheep were, but when you spend hours sitting in the sun watching sheep sleeping in the shade you really begin to wonder about the whole concept of intelligence.

It was a few years later, at a spiritual retreat being led by a fairly well-known Quaker author, that my thoughts on the subject evolved. The group was small, maybe seven or eight people, mostly women and mostly older than me and mostly urban or suburban, but the speaker was dynamic and witty and his books were learned and deep and so we sat around at meals and other times of sharing and listened to his every word.

Letting the discussion draw out after lunch one day, he regaled us with stories of his recent time in Ireland.

"I was staying at a cottage in the countryside writing a book that's coming out soon. It was beautiful," he said, "but the sheep… the sheep were so damn noisy."

He told how in Ireland the sheep graze freely and they would often be grazing around his cottage. The second he went out the door, they'd come running, bleating, and screaming their heads off.

"Sheep are so stupid," he said.

"The only stupid thing," I said, "is to expect a sheep to act like something other than a sheep." The silence was drawn out, telling me I'd committed yet another social faux pas. Like sheep, I often chose to bleat at the wrong time. The author looked stunned and then smiled and laughed.

"I guess I was told," he said. And then, because a challenge can never be resisted. "So, why do they do that?"

I shrugged. "You're a human. What's a human to a sheep but a source of food? And sheep like all of us are always thinking about where and when their next meal is coming from. Why wouldn't they baa at you? It's the only logical thing to do for a sheep."

I'd been that source of food for enough sheep to know that deafening bleating clamor, but I also knew the sweet sound of soft munching that comes from a flock well fed. And the sense of satisfaction that descended from being the shepherd that fed them.

Before starting graduate school, Bruce and I lived at the US Sheep Experiment Station in Dubois Idaho. Dubois was the county seat of Clark County Idaho, a county of 1700 + square miles of sagebrush, 900 people, 4000 cows, and 10,000 sheep. Four-thousands of those sheep lived at the experiment station, where Bruce got a job lambing out ewes one spring. It was 1980, and no one was willing to hire me, a woman, to work at the station.

In the evening after the day shift had all gone home, I'd sneak out with Bruce's dinner and stay the evening helping out. Which was why, on a frigid March night shortly after Bruce and I married, I had my hands inside an ewe's warm vagina trying to convince her twin lambs to take turns coming into the world.

There was a massive tangle of heads and hooves. For a second, feeling around, I thought I was going to have to put a jigsaw puzzle together by feel alone. I took a tiny little cloven hoof between my fingers, and felt the small leg attached to it. Feeling my way along the leg, I found a shoulder, a neck, finally the head that went with that little front hoof. Finding the other leg, I pulled the right set of front legs forward and pushed the second lamb back a little.

Head and legs sorted, the ewe gave a low groan and heaved her sides. The lamb's head flopped out, covered in membranes, wet and bloody. A moment of resistance and then a pop as the lamb's shoulders came through the birth canal. In a rush of amniotic fluid, the rest of the lamb slid out onto the straw. The lamb wasn't breathing.

I wiped the membranes away from its nose and tickled inside one nostril with a piece of straw. It shook its head and sneezed, clearing the fluid out of its passages. The lamb took its first breath and baaed to its mother, who turned her head and answered in a soft low rumble. Bruce put the lamb in front of the ewe, who nuzzled it as she licked it clean. Free of the tangle of its sibling's legs, the second lamb plopped out on its own.

After the lambs were licked off, we got the mother up. The lambs stood on wobbly legs, butting her side as they sought for her udder. Guiding them in the right direction, I stood up and leaned against the pen wall. The lambs latched on, and as the nursed we watched their small tails wag.

"I knew the first time I saw your hands," Bruce said to me, "they'd be good for birthing lambs."

We stood for a long time watching those lambs nurse. Listening to their mother softly talk to them. We watched until they had their belly's full, and their mother laid down, and they curled up tight next to her. As the quiet descended around us, the soft sounds of ewes murmuring to their lambs, or chewing their cuds, or lambs nursing, we watched because it was still the most satisfying thing to do that I knew.

Some knowledge you just fall into. Living in Illinois, Bruce came home from his job at the vet school with an orphaned baby goat. Anabel spent the first weeks of her life in our rented ranch on a suburban street in Urbana, following our dogs around and bawling her head off every time we locked her in the basement. That the neighbors never reported us for child abuse was a miracle. Hopefully, it was because we weren't fooling them that we had a goat in the house and not the screaming baby that she sounded like.

She bounced around the house, boing, boing, boinging her way across the couch, up on the window seat, across the easy chair. By a few weeks old, she had learned to leap up onto the table, sliding across its slick surface and wiping out a centerpiece and some dishes in one swift move. We tried diapers on her, which once wet slid right off her butt, baby goats' butts being rather sloppy. Fortunately, she followed the dogs everywhere and was soon bouncing out the door into the yard to add small goat pellets to the dogs' larger poop piles.

By the time we moved onto Virginia, Anabel had been fostered with a friend who had a pig and had learned to both eat grain, something we and the dogs couldn't teach her, and also to live outside. Still, when once again, Bruce brought an orphaned baby home from work in Virginia, this time a lamb, we brought Anabel back into the house to try to teach Yam, the lamb, the ropes. Also, Anabel didn't like being out in the cold by herself and we were suckers for a crying goat.

Yam started out weak and small and was happy to spend the first days in a cardboard box filled with hay. But within a week, she'd discovered how to jump out and the fun began.

It was the late 1980's, and we'd rented a small place about eight miles out of Blacksburg, VA with an acre or two. The house had two front doors that opened into bedrooms, and two living rooms that had no front door at all. We'd put the couch in the front room, but there was only one dim overhead light, and so we spent our winter evenings in the back living room, sitting on the floor near the woodstove. We had no tv and evenings were spent reading aloud to each other and the dogs, Finn our Golden and Piper our

Border Collie, as they sprawled out around us. Into this mix, we added Anabel and Yam.

Lamb and goat chased each other around the room. Occasionally they bounced over, or on, one of the dogs, who bore it with resigned fortitude. We bought diapers for Yam, which was when we discovered that, unlike goat's, baby sheep have very square butts. Even wet, the diapers stayed on.

One night, as Yam and Anabel raced around the living room, Yam darted behind the wood stove. The space between the wall and the stove was narrow, and for a minute I didn't think she'd fit through, but as she jumped clear the smell of burning plastic filled the room. Her diaper had a large melted hole where she'd brushed against the woodstove on her way through.

"Well, they may stay on," Bruce said, "but they definitely melt."

The next day we built a pen for her, with a heat lamp on the front porch. She still got to come into the house and run around with the dogs, but at night she slept on her porch in the little box and Anabel went out to a pen we'd built her in the yard.

A few days later, drifting off to sleep snuggled between Bruce and Finn, I noticed a light out of the porch. The only light out there was the heat lamp in Yam's box, but it wasn't normally so bright. As I stared, the light grew bright. I got up and peaked out

the window, seeing a definite glow coming from
Yam's box.

I opened the door and stepped out onto the box,
to find flames shooting out the side of the plywood
box. Opening the top of the box, Yam leaped straight
into my arms.

"Bruce," I hollered, "the box is on fire."

Yam apparently had gotten big enough that her
head hit the lamp directing its heat toward the wood.

A three-inch hole had burnt through the crate. The wood had gone from smoldering to actually flaming. We disconnected the lamp, put out the flames and brought Yam inside.

The next day, we decided if she was big enough to burn things down by hitting the heat lamp, she was big enough to keep herself warm. When moved back to upstate NY, our small tribe had grown to thirty sheep and four dogs. When we were looking for a place, the realtor kept asking what style house we wanted.

"The house doesn't matter," we said, "We need a place with land and a barn."

The old farmhouse, with a run-down dairy barn sitting on twenty-five acres that we bought, looked just like what you'd end up with if you said, "we don't care about the house."

Long before the days of high-speed internet or satellite dishes, our options for tv were limited, but with sheep and dogs, we had all the entertainment we needed. We'd walk the dogs up the hill and throw the frisbee. We'd sit and watch the sheep graze and the lambs play. They'd chase each other around, their small legs bouncing as a pod of lambs circled the pasture. Often racing across the run. Occasionally stopping to check on their mothers.

At sunset, we'd watch lambs play and learn to be sheep, and dogs run and learn to be dogs; watching, we learned to be human.

What is it Saint-Exupéry says about the Little
Prince? "The proof that the little prince existed is that
he was charming, that he laughed, and that he was
looking for a sheep. If anybody wants a sheep, that is
proof that he exists."

People have often asked when they hear we had
sheep, "why? Why sheep?"

My standard reply used to be that it was cheaper
than therapy. Now, I have to say it's also more
effective. Cold winter nights out in a barn—
trying to coax a lamb into the world, or convince it to
stay once it's arrived—is living life rather than
ruminating. Watching lambs chase each other across
a field, on a spring evening, has lightened my heart.
Watching lambs play, I've learned to pay attention.
Being with them when they die, I've come to
understand that life includes joy and sorrow, birth and
death. and everything in between. Whether watching
sheep from a roof or a hillside or the porch, life is
richer. Wanting a sheep isn't so much proof I exist, as
it is an act that has made me feel more alive, more
connected to life, and feel like a better human. And
so, I watch, pay attention, and learn.

Priscilla Berggren-Thomas

Rachel Dickinson, art

Sally Stormon, art

A Day Such As This

Yesterday, my friend and I sat
on a porch watching hydrangea
bloom, smelling its distant and distinct sweetness.
Blue Jays, chickadees
and goldfinch swooped
from branches on a River Birch—
making their way to the feeder.
We talked about what we eat
and how we feed our souls—

One way
is by releasing what we cannot control.
And can you predict the next part? Of course.
Controlling the things we can.
And lastly? Being able to tell the difference.
It is not easy.
It is hard.
It is also the only thing that works.

One of the first steps, we agree,
is to do things slow, slow, slowly—
staying present, casting fear
and doubt, not like a net, not
to catch them— but casting
them out and away.

Lisa Harris

Winnowing

August 7, 2025

Is it possible to have a winnowing
of the spirit? Can I learn
to separate the extraneous stalks
from the chaff?

How do I recognize weaknesses
and separate them from strengths?
How do I keep what is necessary
and discard the useless?

In the planter on the porch,
I locate and gather six-inch tall silver maples
who insist upon life wherever they land.

Each year I have admired their tenacity,
and them watch them
as they are mowed down.

This year I have pledged
to dig them out of flower boxes
and gutters, of border gardens
and crevices in macadam.

I am putting them in small
containers and offering them
to passersby, a relocation

project on a scale I can manage.
What if each of us made a choice
to appreciate what is offered to us,
and when we have an abundance,
we make it possible for those
who not only don't have plenty,
but don't even have enough?

What if we shared
the tangible and the intangible?
What if we learned how to love?

Lisa Harris

Gratitude

August 6, 2025

Fog lifts
while dew remains.
I walk, barefoot
and wet-footed
on tender green grass,
at peace with itself.
Grass has a rare consciousness
I barely understand,
but yearn to imitate,
as I aim for peace within myself
despite war, famine, lies,
more lies and endless distortions.
My worst condition is forest
fire smoke
born on the wind and a great
fear of ticks
taking people to their graves.

Peace within begins within
one person at a time,
one instant at a time,
the way a million piece
puzzle begins to
create a picture.

This day present itself
calmly here
with white sunlight
in open spaces as well
as in shadowy hideouts,

filtering through old growth
forests.

I pray
for truth to surface above
lies, for kindness to overshadow
cruelty.

Lisa Harris

Linda Bigness, art

Dust

Tiny particles in the air
some seen and some invisible.
We come from dust
and to dust we return…
a cross-stitch
my aunt made
in a time of tribulation
and before she died, Close
One week ago, Death got
between us, close enough to be
named, refusing to be ignored,
insisting to be taken seriously.
Long ago bite, unseen, untreated
of a tiny tick, ixodes scapularis.
Generally, I don't take much for granted.
Now I see each thing as a gift.
Science and God formed a magic alchemy
that kept me here in this form,
in this world where you keep me looking
at dahlias blooming where you planted them.

Lisa Harris

Sharon Souva, art

Lane Change

I was in a hurry. I'd sandwiched grocery shopping into a busy week that included caring for my elderly parents, babysitting grandchildren, and working a full-time job. I stomped as fast as I could through the slush in the parking lot and grabbed the first available cart, which had three well-oiled wheels and one that made a weird squeaky noise. No matter, I decided, as the cart rattled across the faux brick floor. It wasn't like I was buying the cart.

At the pharmacy counter, I tried (and failed) to sort out a snafu with my mother's prescriptions: medicine for diabetes and dementia. I wasn't worried about the dementia medicine because it didn't seem to work anyhow, but my mother could die without insulin. The manager tried to be helpful but couldn't give me the drugs without a bunch of authorizations. I needed to shop fast, and then go call my mother's doctor and then Medicare.

The grocery cart screeched as I rushed through the aisles. My husband and I used a grocery list app which made choosing food for my household easy. But under glaring overhead lights, I struggled to read the crumpled yellow paper from my 93-year-old father. He'd scribbled his list in pale pencil, and his handwriting was terrible. Heimlich bread? Did he mean Heidelberg bread?

For sixty years, my mother did the grocery shopping, until her dementia forced her removal from the kitchen. My father learned to cook in his 90s, but he didn't grasp the concept of a grocery list, and his list was always incomplete. Milk, for instance. I knew that they needed it, but it wasn't on the wrinkled yellow paper. My father didn't really know how to run a household, although I had to give him credit for trying. I usually checked their refrigerator myself before shopping for them, but today I'd forgotten. So, I had to just guess.

Some days I enjoyed the ritual of buying groceries — choosing vegetables, thumping watermelons, talking to neighbors, buying myself a treat at the candy aisle — but this was not one of those days. I could feel the tension headache beginning. I took a sharp right and wheeled my cart into the first available checkout lane. I dug a handful of re-usable bags out from under the groceries and tossed them onto the conveyor belt. The bags came in garish colors: lime green, bright orange, and deep purple.

The grocery store had many competent cashiers, particularly the older women who had worked there for years, who knew where everything was, and who could punch buttons on the cash register without even looking. I especially liked Debbie, the woman with the ponytail of gray hair, because we usually chatted about the challenges of taking care of elderly parents while she efficiently scanned my items.

But that day the cashier was a teenage boy who stared at the cash register like it was foreign object. Great, I thought. A newbie. It always surprised me that a teenager who could send texts in a flash or spend hours on video games could be so flummoxed by a cash register.

I had done it again. Chosen the wrong lane. I swear, the minute I get into a checkout lane, it screeches to a halt as the cashier turns on her light and calls for a price check.

It was too late to switch lines: there were people behind me. I loaded my groceries efficiently onto the conveyor belt, making sure I put anything heavy in the front so that the hapless kid wouldn't pile canned goods onto bread. I put my parents' groceries in the front and
mine in the back, and I put the little plastic divider thing in between.

"Please ring them up as two separate orders." I waved my hand at the front pile of food. "That stuff is for my parents, and they like the receipt." My father wanted to pay for his own groceries; he clung to that sliver of independence.

I wasn't sure if the teenager heard me. He kept punching numbers into the cash register, one finger at time. This was going to take forever. The teenage boy didn't know the produce codes by heart.

Of course he didn't. This was probably his first week. It turned out he wasn't terribly good at identifying vegetables either.

It's a failure of education, I think. A whole generation who doesn't know their root vegetables. Even the most common type of produce seemed to confuse him.

"That's green leaf lettuce," I said to hurry him along. "The code is 4076. And the red leaf lettuce is 4075."

He looked up from the cash register in surprise. "Do you work here?" he asked. It was a genuine question.

No, I didn't. But when you shop at the same store every week for more than forty years, and you buy almost the same food every single week, you learn the codes. I inserted my credit card and typed the information. Then I turned back to the candy rack to choose a chocolate bar. I needed some comfort food for the upcoming phone call with Medicare. I knew what was coming: me sitting in a parking lot listening to elevator music on my phone while robotic voices put me on hold again and again.

Once he had turned away from the confusing cash register, the teenage boy seemed to perk up. He bagged the groceries with surprising speed and piled them into the cart. He handed me two receipts. "I put your parents' groceries in the purple bags," he said shyly. "And yours in the red bags. That way, you won't mix them up."

This small kindness caught me by surprise. The frantic energy in my brain calmed for just a moment. I stood still, hands on the cart, feet on the floor. The chaos around me — the clanging metal grocery carts, the hum of the registers, the music playing over the speakers — felt suddenly warm and friendly and familiar, filled with humans who were all just trying to buy food, trying to feed their kids or their parents and the people they loved.

I looked at the teenage boy, seeing him for the first time. His name tag read Jeff. He had brown eyes and a nice smile. His haircut was a little jagged at the neck, like perhaps someone had cut it at home.

"Thank you, Jeff." I said. "Thank you."

Janine DeBaise

No Screens In Sight

They call it adventuring
A hike in the woods with mom and the dog.
Explorers, they make up stories on their way.
Carry backpacks with maps, spyglasses, snacks.
They explore places where Washington and his men
camped just before heading to Trenton on Christmas.
They climb the marked boulder where colonial look-
outs once stood and searched the Delaware
downstream looking for the Hessians and other
soldiers. They gather sticks that can morph into
various necessities: a magic wand, a walking stick, a
musket, a sword. On sides of paths strewn with
nature's offerings, detritus to some, lies creative gold
for the young.

Sometimes they end up at Ringing Rocks,
a park where you bring a hammer to tap on diabase
boulders. These taps make ringing sounds come alive
from what appear to be piles of ordinary rock.
The bell-tones call, as you cross the river, the pretend
one, and you signal silently to your leaders
hasten the escape from the bad guys,
could be interlopers or British troops on the march.

Never too cold if dressed in layers and moving,
never too muddy if wearing good rain boots

and warm socks, never any time to be bored or lonely
or mad about a little slight.
Lots of time to be lost in the mystery of a childhood
deliberately spent in nature, walking, pretending,
breathing. Time for hearing the quiet of birdsong
and breathing fresh air.
Arms around one another.
No screens in sight.

Janet Fagal

Snake Skins and Beowulf

I hear him mutter, "Music? Compared to what you listen to? I've got some music you need to hear." We return to my house. He finds music on his phone. "This. This is music."

Large rock casts a wide, dark, shadow on the wet, brown sand. Filaments of color scream through its immensity. Now that, that's a rock. Nothing like that sand over there, meaningless sand.

Sometimes, I stand before the world cowering behind insecurities. I could be at peace if I let myself stay grounded. But I often travel out onto ledges, steep cliffs, slippery slopes of doom. Why go there?

Some people own horses as friends, tall animals with long faces, soft noses, their height measured in hands.

My neighbor is building a greenhouse in his backyard. He'll most likely grow pot. Neighborhood has changed since neighbors died. Esther, Sara, Earl Williams, old man Parker—gone. Esther from Nebraska, Sara's kitchen never updated. Williams shot would-be burglars with his shotgun–didn't hurt 'em, just scared the hell out of 'em. Old man Parker's wife had Alzheimer's. She made no sense when I stopped to admire his chrysanthemums.

What remains of stories? Kindness stays. Laughter
is remembered. Esther had a great laugh. The man
from behind our farm walked for miles across fields.
Showed up in our yard, his pants wet from urine.
He'd ask for a glass of water, then head back home.

Poets chase sounds, sense, sexuality. All the rest is
boring. Who wants to talk about tariffs and taxes and
idiots? I want the middle story, the in-between the
loud noises. I want the lyrical dance, the warmth and
softness of time.

Peepers are sounds on a spring night I hear, while
driving home after book club. Resonating calm,
memories, always reverent, always exciting. Tiny
frogs with swollen necks shout their love to me. I
bow to their music.

Hands on the clock move, regardless of what's being
said, or who is being destroyed, Meanwhile, people
slowly eat supper. Skies change color. Most times,
nobody notices.

There were shelters in the mountains, for Choctaw
children hiding in the woods. Sometimes, I long to
find Carlos Castaneda's Don Juan in the desert. I
want to stand on my head beside him.

Poets need to understand the world,
spend time with pen and paper,
search their brains to make sense of things.
Others drink, gamble, go up in rocket ships
looking for Mars. Poets prefer to plant their feet.

Tell me who I was. Tell you who you are.
Scratched messages slipped into pockets,
written in fancy fonts. How do you feel
when you wake up at 2 AM, your chest sweaty,
your brain screeching around the corner?
Poets want to return there. Dreams confuse.
Memories malleable. News may, or may not, be true.

Look for the animal skins, birds' feathers, empty
cicada shells. Trout hide under bridges and rocks,
so shiny, so shy, seek mayflies. So much seemed
important. I held a big camcorder on my shoulder,
videotaped ceremonies, dances, parties, sacraments,
stored in a tin in the attic, buried beneath trophies,
prom dresses, artwork on construction paper-falling
brittle into pieces like snake skins.

Spoken poetry lasts. The cadence of Beowulf
read in ninth grade, the movement – like music,
still remains in my heart.

Bobbie Dumas Panek

Dale Hutton, art

Appearing at the Schweinfurth Art Center's
Made in New York exhibition

(Used with artist's permission.)

Notes in Hollow Spaces

All seems to be what it's supposed to be. Nature trails
lead to lungs, to hearts, to my muse, my tongue, from
the tips of my fingers. Paths in woods near broken
stone walls, beside railroad bed, lead to music
rushing, under bridges. Notes in hollow spaces,
crumbling foundations where industries used hands
of men and women to sort, assemble, box, design.
Now moss, roots, abound on logs, side hills, around
trees. Ash Borer Beetles decided which trees should
be felled. These small insects took down mighty
trees—with their tiny teeth and weird bodies.
Nothing is ever the same moment to moment. Wind
stirs. Waters fall. Shadows dance. Birds chirp. Ants
carry heavy loads. Mosquitoes buzz. Dogs pull on
leashes. Ivy winds itself up, around, whatever it can.
Grows far and wide, even strangles. It's what vines
do.

Bobbie Dumas Panek

The Body Knows

its own grief. Words we never wished
to acquire. Systems, sinews, psyche.
The joints. Human is a machine with three
pumps, many cisterns. Your heart cycles first,
fills and slackens, exhausted.
A trip—and a fall. A toe. Gravel
under the skin. Little things changed
everything. Grandmother sat, foot in a basin,
Whew, we said. Smelled bad but looked better.
Learn: gangrenous doesn't mean "like your Gran"
Pale skin seamed itself, a cover
for what you don't know...Kind neighbor's call,
strained voice through a taut larynx.
Tears on verge of lids at the sight.
Learn: that debridement
is not about a wedding. This seal
must be broken. Rip off the scabby
mask of health, reveal the work
of microbes in weeping channels.
Gentle sponging gives way.
Harsh scrubbing or a knife,
business-like: what must be done.
Long after antiseptic has wafted away
the sting and reek remain.
Rinse. Repeat. The sight sickens.
The limb looks worse. Aide Rosa pulls

the bandaged scab away, worries
about saving Gran's leg, keeping her job.

Back-of-mind, rent, day care bills. Rosa fusses
over Gran, who plans a gift for Rosa's baby.
Learn: dehisce does not quiet the cat. Stitches
dissolve unsealed. Pain is an open mimosa
leaf, startled by her touch.

Carolyn Ostrander

Angel at Three

(1931)

fell into the flour barrel,
came up clothed in white
powdery cloud, shimmering.
Ellie, digging under shoulders to lift her up,
showered her in words as she rose
worrisome thing—
land-sakes!
no telling what you do next
I declare!
Ellie combed grit from auburn curls to reveal
their own color again, swatted clouds
of evidence from hem and collar, covered telltale
caked seams with sister's pinafore
to save her a licking.
Ellie sent Angel dancing to scatter corn to the chicks
shaking her head. She shut that barrel lid tight
just the same before she turned back to her stove.
That child. No telling at sunup
what Angel would be up to by nightfall.
"Trouble since the day she was born," said Pa.
A real dark tale, that was. Angel born early,
soft bones, mother in malarial coma.
Doctor'd given 'em both up for dead.
Both proved him wrong, though. Stubborn
as each other, no stopping either one!

"Miracle from God," Angel's gran reproved.
Her son, still grieving the near-loss of his wife,
muttered curses. Gran predicted: "that babe will go
far!"
Three years on, Ellie prophesied too—
Drive me into an early grave!

(1933)

By five, Angel was like to elevate the whole house
from its moorings, send it floating down the Cape
Fear.
Older sisters started out good as gold,
but Angel passing by seemed to light a fire
under serious Lou, and pious little Mary Ann too.
Lord only knows what coulda happened
If Ellie hadn't stretched up to hang
a sheet on the line and glimpsed
Three girls
arms up, balancing down railroad tracks,
headed to cool off under trees by the river.
Quicksand by the banks. Lord only knows!
And all those gals could say was. "Angel said—"
Oh, It was cool by the river. They'd only
dip their toes. Ellie, frightened as she was
angry, stopped them.
Forget what Angel said,
What's your Pa gonna say?
The next week Pa found them three,

adding precious eggs to a mudpie
to stir it up smoother. And he had plenty
to say then too. Lean times mean nothing's
extra. Idle hands are the devil's playthings.
Not two days, Angel went to fighting with Lou,
flinging hard corn cobs at each other and
ducking down behind corners of the crib.
All that while they should have been tying
tobacco to hang in the drying shed.
Working's next to godliness.
Never where you want her, that child.

(1938)

Angel at ten rocked forward and back
pretending to be in the porch swing:
crossed feet, elbows on knees,
hands over her face, seat on a pew.
Eyeing strangers between spread fingers,
fidgeting at the Mission Society meeting. Tsk!
Visiting man was telling his good works
and life amongst Cubanos. His wife silent
beside him like a statue. Missionary girls,
older, attentive and still,
clasped Bibles in their hands.
Once, twice, the younger leaned close
to whisper in Sister's ear.
Reverend Pa asked his daughters for a hymn
Angel sat up, something new in the air.

Two girls rose arm in arm, harmonized
in Spanish with refrain in plain English.
Angel never looked away.
Bees strayed through open windows
Severe ladies ducked blossom-decked hats
as questing insects buzzed close. Church fans
raised like bids cards at a cattle auction.
Boys behind her snickered. Angel didn't hear.
Still as a mannequin for the rest of the service.
Mother was grateful. Ellie might've asked
if Angel was taking sick. That still. Quiet
all the ride home too.
Taking biscuits from the oven, Ellie turned
caught sight of her lanky and wayward charge
ramrod straight under pecan trees, staring
at something beyond the lane. Angel's
silhouette or the way shadows
played around her made Ellie shiver.
First time I knew, she'd grow up and left.

Carolyn Ostrander

This Little Light Of Mine

In 2006, I spent nearly a month touring China with my mother. We settled on a tour that would take us to the Great Wall, to the terra-cotta warriors, to Hong Kong. But, most importantly, we would get a three-day stop in Lhasa, the capital of Tibet.

As a native of nearby Tompkins County, I grew up with a sense of Podunk-familiarity for Tibet. The Namgyal monastery looked like any other house downtown, and in the winter, the Buddhist monks wore puffy down jackets over their hot orange robes. Ithaca prided itself as the Dalai Lama's official North American seat which, for a long time, I thought was a joke about butts. So, when we were prepping for the trip to Lhasa, all I could think was: mountains? Monks? No problem.

I was a white American girl in a state-approved tour group, so the glimpse of Lhasa I was given was brief and curated. But we did get to climb to the Potala Palace which is, historically, the Dalai Lama's winter residence. The sprawling construction sits at over 12,000 feet above sea level—the highest palace on earth. We had to climb the road to the palace at a snail's pace so we didn't get altitude sickness.

But when we finally reached the palace... that view. Wow. Nothing beats the Himalayas at enforced perspective: I felt like a speck, a nothing—no better

or worse than everything else that wasn't the mountains and the sky. I was on the roof of the world, and I felt my head brush up
against something larger and lighter.

For a second, I got it. I thought of my hometown monks, hiking the gorges and hills that I now realized were quaint, probably even claustrophobic for the Tibetans in Ithaca. I tried to picture Dalai in the palace, rather than his house-turned-monastery. I tried to picture him at all, but all images of the Dalai Lama are outlawed in Tibet for being too political.

A massive stretch of pavement sits below the Palace, facing it, with a towering, hundred-foot concrete monument rising imperiously at the end.

This "Monument to the Peaceful Liberation of Tibet" is, aesthetically-speaking, unlike anything around it: spare, severe, imposing and sharp. Even against the dramatic background of the Himalayan mountains, the monument is an unavoidable sight from the palace, raising a giant middle-finger to the weathered serenity of its surroundings.

After the Palace, we went on a home-visit to have afternoon (yak-butter) tea with a local family. The faces of smiling kids and long-dead ancestors dotted the ledge of their mantle, but they were all dwarfed by a huge, black and white framed photo of men wearing strained smiles. The men: the previous

Dalai Lama, the current His Holiness, and Mao
Tsetung. The photo, from 1955, is the only image of
the Dalai Lama that is allowed to be displayed, and
only because Mao is in it.

Joan Applebaum, art

I went to bed early that night. The haunting drone of the palace ceremonial horns bounced off the mountainsides and reverberated in my head. I remember crying the day we left. It was like having to say goodbye to a dream.

So, I carried a resentment home in Dalai's name, upset that he could never go back to Lhasa because of politics. I was incensed, and less than a year later, I was gearing up to graduate from college, armed with know-how but fueled by spit and ire.

But through cosmic happenstance, my school hosted a special guest that spring: my pal, the Dalai Lama. I was in the glee club, and we were the "entertainment." I'd been mad at the world on Dalai's behalf—defiantly so. And this angry energy carried me to the stage, all the way up to the back riser with the other tall girls until I was about twelve feet from the central dais.

And suddenly, there he was – out of arm's reach, but close enough that I could see a smudge on his glasses. I'd thought of him in Ithaca, I'd thought of him in Tibet, and now he was here.

Hello, Dalai.

The glee club sang a jazzy version of "This Little Light of Mine," which I'd thought was a kind of a goofy choice. But as I clapped and bopped with the rest of the group, I found myself belting right to His Holiness, testifying. His small, knowing smile

widened into a toothy grin, and his eyes sparkled—
the man radiated joy. Defiantly so.

And his light did shine. So brightly, that I
suddenly felt how small and trite my anger really
was.

The Dalai Lama lost everything, then spent
his life being defiantly grateful, radically joyful. I'd
been sheltered and privileged and short-sighted, but I
was shown that delight is empowering, and kindness
is punk.

This is the lesson I've learned, and the best
form of defiance I can offer at the moment: keep your
happiness, and keep it sacred. Because nothing takes
the wind out of desperation's sails as quickly as
smiling joy.

Railey Jane Savage

The Erie Canal Song Doesn't Mean What You Think It Does, The complicated, truth behind one of America's most beloved folk songs.

I've got an old mule and her name is Sal
Fifteen years on the Erie Canal

So, begins "Low Bridge," informally known as The Erie Canal Song, an irresistibly catchy homage to a happy-go-lucky pack animal on America's most famous inland waterway. You remember singing it as a kid, right? Maybe your teacher showed you a book with a picture of a mule-drawn packet boat gliding through the bucolic Upstate New York countryside.

"It was the ditch that built America!" she may have said, and she was right. The 363-mile Erie Canal transformed U.S. transportation almost overnight, reducing travel time from Albany to Buffalo from four weeks to just six days. It enabled western expansion and immigration, opened up new markets for American goods, and made New York City the #1 port city in the country. Today, three-quarters of the population of Central and Western New York still lives within 25 miles of the original canal.

"A gathering place for scum and refuse." But just as the Erie Canal eclipsed the stagecoach, so the faster, cheaper, more comfortable railroad eclipsed the canal. By the time Thomas S. Allen wrote "Low

Bridge" in 1905, the canal's golden years were long behind it.

Traffic was largely limited to hauling materials the railroads didn't want to handle, like gravel and coal. Even the "Low bridge, ev'rybody down" in the chorus had a grim backstory. Passengers riding on top of the boat had to fling themselves facedown on the deck when passing under a low bridge, or risk being scraped off into the water, or even crushed to death.

And the mules? Once beloved for their patience and stamina, mules began disappearing from the towpath in the late 1800s, replaced by steam barges that didn't need to be rested, fed or driven. By the dawn of the 20th century, New York State had begun building a wider, deeper Barge Canal, sans animal power, to accommodate larger vessels and remain competitive in the shipping industry.

Thomas Allen finally copyrighted his composition in 1912. Five years later, the Erie Canal closed for good. Unlike the old boatman in Low Bridge, very few people at the time mourned its passing.

In Syracuse, for example, where newspapers had long characterized the canal as "a menace to public health"; and "a gathering place for scum and refuse;" residents rejoiced as the "old sore" that had divided their city was filled in and became Erie Boulevard.

So, what's the Erie Canal Song really about?
The overall meaning of "Low Bridge" changed quite
a bit between its first publication and its reintroduc-
tion in the 1960s. Just look at some of the original
lyrics:

We'd better look 'round for a job old gal
Fifteen years on the Erie Canal
You bet your life I wouldn't part with Sal
Fifteen years on the Erie Canal
Once a man named Mike McGinty tried to put
it over Sal.
Now he's way down at the bottom of the Erie
Canal
A friend of mine once got her sore
Now he's got a broken jaw
'Cause she let fly with her iron toe
And kicked him back to Buffalo.

With its evocations of unemployment,
violence, and murder, it's not exactly the version
trilled by generations of schoolchildren, is it? It's
unclear when the lyrics changed, or who changed
them. Chances are, it wasn't anyone who actually
worked on the canal. The switch from "Fifteen years"
to "Fifteen miles" is especially rich, considering
canal boats ran day and night, stopping only to take
on supplies, switch out mules, or make repairs. Most
boats could easily cover 50 miles or more per day.

What's clear is that at some point, someone decided the reverie of a long-time "canaler" mourning a dying industry should be reincarnated as nostalgia. By the time Pete Seeger introduced "Low Bridge" during the folk-revival movement of the 1960s, almost all the old boatmen had passed away, and much of the original waterway had been filled in or abandoned.

The song was immediately embraced by a new generation of mostly young, mostly idealistic Americans yearning for a time when life unfolded at the pace of a packet boat gliding gently toward the next town.

It would later be recorded by artists ranging from Bruce Springsteen to Suzy Bogguss, and remains a staple of school sing-alongs.

If the youngsters in your life come home singing with shining eyes about a mule named Sal, please don't burst their bubble. But you might want to look up the version sung by Rochester folk performer Dave Ruch on YouTube, featuring all five original verses. Once the kids hear the whole story about Sal's pugnacious personality, they may decide they like her even more.

Kimberly Parr

The Rope

I.
Shadows distort
against the rock
face
arms and legs are
spider long
spinning
a single thread.
Though I helped
to coil a rope
broader
than my thumb,
know the weight
it will sustain.

Still, I think it looks
as if the spiders
spun
or were spun by it –
my palms sweat.

Safe at the rocky
base, I
can't watch
directly.
Focus on shadows:

not resembling
loved ones,
can't be hurt by a
fall,
betrayed by rope.

My friends reach a
ridge
with shouts and
laughter.
The rope that held
is gathered
up. Proud climbers
disappear
around an outcrop.

II.
In the distance a
spot
moves up the wall
a trick of light,
the line of sight
or the way he
clings:
this one not
distended,
clearly a man.
No thread bobbles

below no rigging.
No net. Look ma,
only hands and toes
and faith in the
rock.

Climb higher;
will you be more
secure?

My heart pounds
thinking
of ground below.

Thoughts see
treetops,
cars in the distance.
Lone hawk soaring
at eye level:
See how small we
are! Face upturned,
eyes straining to
add to the will that
defies gravity.

The free climber
slowly, cautiously
considers the next
move.

III.
The difference
between
climbing with a
rope
and climbing free
parts me from
myself.
I ache to be
a free climber
daring dizzying
heights,
looking out but
never down.
Why see where you
will fall?

But me: I want to
rig the ropes and
know
they hold if I
misjudge
the reach,
the ledge,
the drop,
the one I count on
to belay my fall.

**Carolyn
Ostrander**

Joan Applebaum, art

**Like voters heading to the polls,
we travel free**

*Pine Creek Gorge Rails to Trails, looking from
Tiadaghton, PA northwest toward Owasee Road*

The cyclist thinks it's a new discovery. Path on cinders,
clean, straight, level, a river bank that is less pristine on
the unmowed bank. Overgrown with willowy aspens
and invasive species, bamboo-like water-lovers with
deceptively horticultural spiky white blooms, insistent
they have nothing to do with how rhizomes claw and

tendrils spread and lock, choking out tender bloodroot, wild iris, jewelweed and approaches to a meandering stream.

Every year, restless waters weave a less certain path around shrub thickets, islets of intruders. They bog down in a stew of water-rooted loosestrife, water hyacinth, water chestnut, water lettuce, the lotus-like floaters that drink and detour flow until defeated currents limp and slink aimless among rushes and under floating tufts of grass.

When they do break free, currents are relentless, angrily lash out, undercut their own banks to reveal lace-worked secondary roots of pin and topple uneven shootlings from sliding hillsides: short-lived birch rotting from trunk to twig's tip; last scions of ancient hemlocks whose house-like stumps are gone to humus, marked only by the smoke of puffballs spores.

A trail is not like a stream, that wanders and fits where it can. It is a full-scale map of the line of thought surveyors' drafts designed, denying the up and down of mountainsides, whose lowest points are at times more seam than valley; steep sides erased, debunked, switched-back, built-up, blasted, cut, hammered out, hair-pinned and hollowed into tunnels otherwhere.

Only in the broad shoulder where a wilder, younger river once thrashed and roared and wore its own cuts down, down through a gorge—only here the track pretends to be landscape. Each hiker, biker, rower, rider saunters safely along, imagining a placid environment with no hint of the savage, desperate tug and pull of energy, light and air for very existence.

Carolyn Ostrander

Joan Stier, art

Catastrophizing is my jam.

My mind can leap from a news headline to being homeless, destitute, and starving on the street in a simply leap across a single synapse. It takes less than a millisecond.

It's not hard now for any of us to catastrophize the situation. Our lives have become precarious. Each new executive order makes us imagine a stock market crash, a roundup of citizens into detention camps, a planet ending in a conflagration. It's easy to just want to go back to the days when our democracy felt stable – like it was working. Or at least for us middle-class white folks, it was working, but even before the current administration came into power, things weren't really working for many people.

Many days it's hard not to despair, to feel hopeless. Joanna Macy and Chris Johnstone, in their book *Active Hope: How to Face the Mess We're in Without Going Crazy* wrote, "Active Hope is a practice. Like tai chi or gardening, it is something we do rather than have. It is a process we can apply to any situation, and it involves three key steps. First, we take a clear view of reality; second, we identify what we hope for in terms of the direction we'd like things to move in or the values we'd like to see expressed: and third, we take steps to move ourselves or our situation in that direction. Since Active Hope doesn't require our optimism, we can apply it even in areas where we feel hopeless. The guiding impetus is intention; we choose what we aim to bring about, act for, or express. Rather than weighing our chances and proceeding only when we feel hopeful, we focus on our intention and let it be our guide."

To this, Kelly Hayes and Mariame Kaba add, "To practice Active Hope we do not need to believe that everything will work out in the end. We need to only decide who we are choosing to be and how we are choosing to function in relation to the outcome we desire and abide by what those decisions demand of us." (From *Let This Radicalize You: Organizing and the Revolution of Reciprocal Care*)

But what exactly does that look like? How would I live if I acted to bring about the world I want to see? First, I have to envision what that world could be.

I want a world that isn't warming, that isn't losing twenty species a day, as many as Americans are losing rights each day. I want a world where we realize we are interconnected to all things and live accordingly.

I want a world not controlled by rich, white, "Christian" men whose goals seem to be to keep everyone else destitute, oppressed, and controllable. I want an end to the white-supremacist patriarchy.

I want a world without misogyny, racism, homophobia, ableism, and xenophobia. I want a world that is intersectionally feminist, filled with equity and justice.

I want a world where happiness is measured in moments with friends, in nature, in cooking a good meal, not in productivity and dollars and cents. I want a world that is communal and natured based, not materialistic and consumer-based.

How, I keep wondering, can I divorce myself from a system that isn't working, from an unjust and harmful society? Learning how to divorce myself from our society's current values and live with my own is much harder (or I am much weaker) than I seem able to do. Capitalism and the resultant materialism drives much of climate change, income inequality, poverty, worker oppression, even sexism and racism.

"Buy less or buy secondhand," is the call to action that environmentalists tell us, and I commit to that mentally, only to find myself looking online at the utility pants I like because I just need to have one more pair in khaki, and they don't sell them at the thrift store. There's that little surge of serotonin when I hit buy, which is addictive and also a temporary distraction from the chaos in our current world, even as my purchase likely contributes to the chaos.

We have a sugar maple in our yard: the largest tree we have. It was tall thirty years ago when we moved here. A branch fell off twenty years ago in a windstorm, and the cavity it left housed a nest of mergansers one spring. This summer a litter of raccoons took up residence in the cavity. Indigo Buntings nest in its branches, and every year the kestrel fledglings use it to fly back and forth from as they test their wings.

I'm trying to imagine myself, our world, our society, our country as a tree and imagining how I can live and grow into that reality.

Can we offer shade and shelter; nourishment and care to others simply because it's who we are? To resist this political regime requires action, but it also requires community and caring. We have to build the world we want, one revolutionary act of defiant kindness at a time.

Priscilla Berggren-Thomas

Reflections

In the mirror
I call out to her.
Her reflection, so youthful.
Eager, hopeful.
I call to her, warn her.
It goes by so fast.
I whisper,
stick your toes in the water!
Do it now.
Jump in with every part of you!
Hurry. Swim hungrily,
voraciously,
into the deep.

Janet Fagal

The Perfect Crime

The foreman stood guard, motionless, finger readied and in position to squeeze the trigger on two mob soldiers. He knew they did not want this job, but they were on the payroll for a reason. It would mean their lives if they refused or failed.

"Throw another log on that fire. It's gotta be hotter," barked the foreman. Waving folded newspapers to stoke the fire, the thugs could only glance at one another, speaking with their eyes. Smoke snaked up the base of a Greek column that served as a support for a former cathedral. Nearby columns continued to buttress what was left of a grand church. The abandoned sacred ground would have been a perfect place to commit a crime had it not been for a full moon. The foreman hardly planned on its bright spotlight and the sky's dissipating clouds.

"Hurry, we haven't got all night." The men worked faster.

In the distance, a young couple romantically chased one another up and down the steps of a gothic pavilion that surrounded the demolished church. Spotting them, the foreman froze, hoping that the unsuspecting interlopers would pivot in another direction.

"They're too far away to notice the fire," he thought. "If they come any closer, I'll have to kill five people tonight." Mercifully, the young lovers disappeared into the night.

The men tossed another log onto the fire and stepped back, protecting themselves from the raging inferno. They lit cigarettes and paused to stare at the blaze as they exhaled. The foreman stood quietly to allow a final moment.

"It's time," said the foreman, "get him out of the car." Taking their last drag, the men flicked their cigarette butts into the fire and headed for the car's trunk. On the trunk's floor, a rolled carpet tied on either end lay behind extra logs. They lifted the cumbersome bundle and dropped it at the foreman's feet, then unrolled the carpet as the hog-tied man spun around. His neck was sliced by a piano wire. With eyes still bulging and glass shards caught in his pant cuffs, it was apparent that he fiercely struggled before succumbing. Two bullets were pumped into his skull.

"Wow, the SOB must have kicked out the windows in the car! Quite the whack job," chuckled a soldier. A hitman who killed targeted men with all kinds of weapons, he had to admire the assassin's technique. He promoted his own line of work by stating that he "painted houses.

If a mobster wished to eliminate a rival, he would send the hitman a cryptic message asking if he painted houses. Adding, "I also need carpentry work," meant to dispose of the bodies. In a clandestine meeting, the two parties negotiated the hit's details.

Anxious to complete the job, the foreman barked, "Now finish him off in the fire. Leave no remains." One worker grabbed the dead man's feet; the other held its head after smashing all the corpse's teeth. They swung him into the pyre and watched the fire crackle and devour his clothing and flesh. Neither knew the famous man's identity, nor did they realize that this murder would never be solved.

*

A history note regarding the real-life incident behind this story's speculations about how Hoffa died: over the past fifty years, law enforcement followed false leads to dig up the victim's body. A movie depicting Hoffa's unscrupulous life rejuvenated interest and suppositions about his death. His body was never found, and it took a court order to declare him "presumed dead."

Jimmy Riddle Hoffa, General President of the International Brotherhood of Teamsters from 1957-1971, disappeared on July 31, 1975 from the parking lot of the Machus Red Fox Restaurant near Detroit, Michigan. He waited in the restaurant for a meeting with two mobsters. That was the last time Hoffa was seen.

Hoffa rocketed the Teamsters into the largest labor union in the United States. "You got a problem? Call me. Pick up the phone," was supposedly Hoffa's rallying cry to his rank-and-file members.

At first, Hoffa's suspected alliance with the mafia was strong. They appeared to help him run undesirable unionists out of town, even execute them, some evidence suggests. In return, it is believed, Hoffa loaned the mob some Teamster funds for casino investments.

What is known is that Hoffa was sentenced to ten years in prison in 1971 for jury tampering, fraud, and conspiracy. He was released from prison by President Nixon after serving only four years. Nixon prohibited Hoffa, however, from any union activity for ten years.

Russell Bufalino, a Pennsylvania mafia head, thought the mob was better off without Hoffa and supported the President's ten-year restriction. However, Hoffa openly began talking about retaking control of the Teamsters. Bufalino feared that he could not control Hoffa and worried Hoffa would rat to Nixon about Bufalino's likely racketeering and persuade the President to lift his constraint. Allegedly, Bufalino ordered hit men to whack Hoffa.

Nixon's Committee to Reelect the President categorically denied receiving a reported donation from the Teamsters of $500,000-$1,000,000.

Karen Foresti Hempson

Rachel Dickinson, art

Untact

These were once
my *keywords*:
dactylic hexameter
epic poetry
Homeric heroes
word cadences
lost pitch of song

And my precious digs?
Nausikaa, a princess,
washing, singing
the river clean:
laughter matrilineal.

Now far gone are
those shining epithets,
patronymics too,
replaced by machines.
Today, editing, I find a new word
freshly flagged: *untact* (stet).
Coined in South Korea,
it evokes "intact,"
a dream economy where
distance-workers, Covid-free,
keep pace with automation:
no touch, no share;

not breath, not smell, nor taste.
You can work from anywhere.

But as dirty laundry, plastics,
acronyms, all keep piling up
in swirling islands somewhere in the Pacific,
there's a vision of a new world
with more and more AI – artificial intelligence –
- ai, ai, ai, - how quickly we mourn losses.

Who will take in clothes and shrouds, fresh, sun-dried?
Estuaries, will they ever again be clean?
Who will greet the heroes coming home?
And Nausikaa? Who knew her name
meant all along: "the burner of ships?"

Carolyn Clark

If I ever was

Forever, if I ever was
is nothing, when once it goes
it's gone.

Life, an endless summer, chases dreams to the edges of
the earth
while death, the endless winter, watches in stillness all
around.
Two seasons bound by a breath.
Life, the tide takes out
a memory, the waves bring back in.

*

Standing on an abandoned rocky shore
wind in hair
shells on toes
thoughts in future
heart in past.

The next season recedes,
a million tiny bursting bubbles tickle my inner ear.
Gone are my fears.

One final longing fills my lungs,
and I open my eyes to another peaceful dawn.

Laura Thorne

Artemis Dream,
Opening Day of Hunting Season

Shotgun shot
wakes me from a dream
so suddenly that
I lose it,
trailing off, into light
so blonde it must be dawn.

Opening Day of Hunting Season.

In a flash I invoke *Potnia Theron*
(Queen of Wild Animals, once the mighty
Ishtar – Nana on Lion – Aphrodite).
Sole Artemis, guardian of deer.
After her demise, her roles fragmented
into a down-sized figurine: archer or bather
by woodland pools where water runs swift as wind.

Goddess of the chase and chastity,
somehow, she knows
birth pangs, the pain of another's labor.

Her preferences? Solitary company,
or perhaps a small circle of young girls.

Hasten, shadows, ferns and gullies.
No Tinker Bell she:
heliotropic
in the forest canopy, gleaning
sunshine wherever it falls, filters.

One loud shot, then another, buckshot,

followed by footfalls (each shoe
a *cauda* (tail) repeating itself,
as if a coda, colon or semicolon)
in the woods of our neighboring gorge.

Who would dare go there today?
Even our black dog stays close,
points, sniffs around the woodpile,
smells death and smoke wafting up from the gulf
while I linger inside, sipping coffee
till these gunshots at last subside, fade off
to the shuffle of my moccasin slippers.

But I promise myself
at night to look up her lovers –

disloyal Orion, or those who espied,
like Actaeon,
all whose stories are written in the stars,

while all the while
Artemis keeps on trying
to protect her wild animals,
desires only

to keep them wild,
wild and far away –
procul harum –
far from these things.

Carolyn Clark

Planet Earth Hanging

Imagine our Earth
a Globe hanging, trembling, quivering –
patches of color like a Crayola box spilled,
not merely blue and green and yellow.
Imagine our Earth
a Globe hanging, trembling, quivering –
forests and lakes, vineyards, fields in bloom,
cultivated farms and fields gone fallow,
fungi, flora and arboreal systems at work under forest
floors, manicured lawns and wildflowers wild
and cultivated.
Imagine our Earth
a Globe hanging, trembling, quivering –
whole landscapes as far as the eye can see:
floods, hurricanes, tornadoes, monsoons and tsunamis;
fire billowing over hills, forests, homes and barns;
the silence of drought, of scorched land smoldering.
Imagine our Earth a Globe hanging, trembling,
quivering–the weight of feet on the move,
the well and the unwell,
leaving the known in tears, in terror, yet resolute,
seeking something better, seeking to be…
because to stay is to lose everything,
to lose hold of hope, of oneself,
to disappear.
Imagine.

Mary L. Gardner

Mary Raineri, art

(turned for larger image)

The Gentle Arts

The other day a friend of mine used the term rage-quitting, and because my head is largely still stuck in 1999, I wasn't familiar with the phrase. I thought she said rage-quilting. I thought about that for a while—imagining the awesome quilt I'd make, wondering if the awesomeness of the quilt was directly proportional to the rage I felt. I have a lot of rage.

Later that night, I wondered if perhaps the phrase should be broadened. Thinking I should stick with the needle arts at which I am moderately skilled, rage-crafting would encompass quilting, knitting, and needlepoint. Maybe even tatting.

I am most adept at rage-knitting. I've been doing it for years. About two decades ago, I told all the kids and my husband to prepare for a Walton Family Christmas. I initially made the pronouncement because I was so sick of all the crap the kids wanted from Santa. But when I think back to that time, I know the real reason was that I was broke. The diatribe against commercialism was a way to recast the I-cannot-afford-to-spend-$100-per-kid-times-four truth of our life in the Pink House back then.

Back then, in my early rage-knitting days, we were watching videotapes of the first couple of seasons of *The Waltons*, the show from the 1970s about an Appalachian family during the Great Depression. I love the first couple of seasons. If you watch with attention—you can discount the long cloying shot that concluded each episode, where the camera pulls back, and you see the exterior of the house with the front porch and stars twinkling in the black, black Virginia sky, and you hear all the children and the parents say good night to one another from the various bedrooms ("good night, Mama; good night, John-Boy; good night, Mary Ellen," and so forth)—you'll meet a family replete with wonderfully complicated relationships. John-Boy, played by Richard Thomas, is desperate to grow up, get off the family farm, and go to college to learn to be a writer. He puts on his round wire-rim glasses and writes in his journal at night before going to bed. Most days, he is aspiring and pretentious; he's human. The rest of the family is similarly troubled in routine ways. The seven barefoot kids walk to school on the dusty road. They bicker and pick on one another. Jealousies flare, and alliances are made and broken and remade. John-Boy, the oldest, yells at all of them. Mary Ellen, the oldest girl, yells back. It is family.

I think my kids were fascinated by the everyday poverty, much the way I was when I first watched the show. Christmas for the Waltons meant presents were made or bought for fifteen cents at Ike Godsey's general store. There were no Volcano Blowouts or Happenin' Hair Barbies under the scraggly tree cut down and dragged home from the woods. Knit scarves and sweaters and hats and little wooden boxes and chairs and very cheap bottles of perfume all changed hands. All those Waltons liked what they received.

Somehow, I knew my kids wouldn't like their handmade gifts. That didn't stop me from doing that first Walton Family Christmas. I knitted pathetic scarves for my children, although that was not my intention. I had grown up with a knitting mother and watched as sweaters took shape with the industrious click-clack of her needles. Not that my mother didn't go through her own craft phases. There was the sixties, and her angels made from folded Reader's Digest magazines with Styrofoam heads then spray-painted gold. And who could forget her sophisticated Williamsburg phase in the seventies when she stuck cloves in rows on oranges then set them on the mantel to shrivel. She wasn't particularly crafty, but she tried. She could, however, knit up a storm. So, I assumed, wrongly, that there was a genetic code for knitting that I surely had inherited.

I bought lovely skeins of wool in various shades of heather and knitting needles, and then I cast on my stitches for a scarf. I didn't count the stitches because it didn't occur to me to do so. I thought you just kept knitting until the scarf was long enough.

I could soon tell the first scarf I worked on was pathetic, yet I could not seem to stop. When I sat down to knit, I would tense up, and every stitch showed a variation in tension—too tight, too loose—and my creations were simply terrible. I used expensive wool. Then I tried cheap acrylic yarn. It didn't matter. Each time the end result was a wreck. The rational side of my brain said, *put down the needles and walk away*. The irrational side wouldn't let me do that. It dawned on me that while I was knitting, I was thinking, and clearly any tension or problem in my little world showed up in my projects. The puzzling part is that I kept knitting, producing four, ill-formed scarves.

On Christmas Day, the kids opened their presents from me—uneven scarves in shades of gray (for that's what heather really is). They were all on the verge of tears, and I could read the thought bubbles over their heads: *Why me?* and *All I wanted was a nine-dollar Barbie.*

Spurred on by my initial failures, I began to furtively watch people knitting in public places. Those people could knit and talk. All I wanted to do was knit, in silence, one decent scarf. I then watched a YouTube video about knitting and discovered I was knitting backwards.

At one point I abandoned my needles and took up needlepoint. It seemed like the only skill needed was the ability to count. I could do that. (I could even do algebra if it was required because I was reading *Algebra for Dummies* so I could help one of my kids pass the course.)

I imagined re-creating medieval tapestries complete with scenes of gentlewomen holding fierce falcons on their gloved fists. Or I could make something simpler, like a small piece consisting of intertwined Celtic designs. These pieces would be like works of art and would take more concentration than the knitting, meaning I might keep my tension-inducing, rage-producing thoughts at bay.

Fail. I had discovered another rage-craft. Did you know that needlepoint also shows tension? That it's hard to do and that the requisite skills go beyond basic counting? And that there's a reason you don't see a whole lot of it around because it takes f o r e v e r to complete one project? I made pincushions decorated with the most uncomplicated Celtic design I could find. When I finished, I realized that the color combinations were terrible—weak mustard and watery blue—and the final products looked like mistakes from the nineteenth century but lacking the nostalgia that can make poor craftsmanship appealing. And who even uses a pincushion? My therapist suggested I was really making voodoo dolls. Perhaps.

Fast-forward to fifteen years of rage-crafts littering my house. Some are so bad—like the red-and-purple-striped scarf that both gains and loses stitches in unequal proportions I knitted after my son died—that they remain hidden at the bottom of bags holding balls of yarn. Worse, for my family, some poor pieces are in dresser drawers or propped up on bookshelves as pathetic displays of my craftiness.

I've tried to analyze my behavior. First, what compels me to embark on these projects? Then, where did I go wrong? My projects encapsulate both technical and psychological problems. To untangle these might take years.

I think the impulse is good (although my children might disagree as they open yet one more failed project each Christmas). Intellectually, there is a desire to keep the gentle arts alive. Realistically, my projects prove that the Industrial Revolution happened for a reason—not everyone could keep their family clothed and warm by their own hand.

The practical problem lies in what's going on in my head when I'm doing these projects. I suspect most people use knitting as a way to relax and don't think about much of anything while they're doing it. Or they're knitting by muscle memory and are watching television or talking while their beautiful, even stitches flow like a gentle waterfall from their needles.

Rather than taking me out of my head, these crafty projects put me squarely in whatever part of the brain controls the emotions. Every project, stitch by stitch, describes the death of my mother and the death of my son. They show money anxieties and dark depressions. They express my desire to withdraw from a world of people where I have to make small talk and be engaging. They exemplify my struggle to maintain human connections.

The scariest projects, at least to me, like the red-and-purple scarf and a half-finished needlepoint project of red poppies, are pure rage. Rage about things that are out of my control. Rage at the things that can't be undone. These projects lie hidden in the Pink House but not destroyed.

Now that my children are older, they've grown more tolerant of the projects they receive on Christmas morning. I think they're beginning to understand that this is my personal therapy. Jokes are made. Mittens the size of catcher's mitts are tried on then quietly placed in the pile of handmade items from Mommy that will never be used. I also notice that they make no effort to discard these pieces. Now, as adults, they recognize each is a record of something important and unnamable.

This year I was thinking of trying quilting—I have a vision of how beautiful the quilt will be with its luscious jewel tones in velvet—but then I remember that I'd be cutting a million pieces of fabric. I can already see the path leading to my failure. The sewing would give me way too much time to go into my head, inevitably producing the five-hundred-hour project known as the rage-quilt. If I could create a quilt as beautiful as the crazy quilts made by lonely women on the prairie, I would gladly put in the time.

These gentle arts seem to be how women have always shown their fury, depression, loneliness, and rage. Their outlet was in the work of their fingers, and the results can often seem like controlled—very controlled—craziness. (Have you ever seen petit point?) Like them, I have the desire to create but lack the skill to produce in practical form what lies locked in my mind.

Maybe it's time to set aside the needles and thread. I don't trust myself with a band saw or whittling knife, so maybe I'll make miniature Adirondack chairs out of wooden clothespins (I bought one of those for five bucks from a guy on the street) or scale replicas of Greek Revival houses from craft sticks. My hope is that working with wood and glue won't tap into the deep well of emotions accessed by the needle arts. Maybe, just maybe, summer camp projects will make me happy and clear my mind.

Rachel Dickinson

Self-Talk, A New Place
After Edward Hopper, Automat 1927

I came up on the train today.
This is my wish, my dream, my tears disappearing
into the rain sliding across the windows.
Everything I know passes behind me, out of view –
wetlands of tall grasses and cattails,
geese resting before their long journeys,
barns and rooflines made for each other fading away
into houses with small yards, fences by the tracks,
smoke stacks and streetscapes crowding out the sky.
The train's brakes slow us out of the wind, its
underbelly groaning and clanging, loud and insistent.
We lurch to a stop.
People are getting off and on,
chasing dreams or sleepwalking through another day.
We're moving again, faster, faster.
A lone whistle trails behind us, sighing into the wind,
mysterious yet knowing, like a keeper of tales,
mine, too. Dropping speed, we screech through
another tunnel, then under the station roof with
its broad bed of tracks, my stop. Nothing like where I
have been, but where I am now; where I will be.
I must take it all in, let it become a part of me,
how I will walk and talk and carry myself.
I take this table near the door, a straight-back chair,
cross my knees.

Where shall I set my eyes, my hands, my yellow
chapeau? Can I make this work?
Will the power of the dream hold me,
enfold me, sustain me, here, in this new place?

Mary L. Garnder

Ovum Suite

1. *Shell*
Simple element, this thin cast of calcium.
Sharp grit on the tongue. Slowly breaking
down in the compost. The persistent
evidence underfoot, or crack of bone
between teeth.

The terrible echo of a tooth falling
into your palm, absolved
of holding on any longer.

We carry on through the day, brittle
reminder of mortality itself, perhaps,
hatching new schemes, or settling
into nests of our own to sleep.

2. *Egg*
Genocide in the hen house

A fetching nourishment
both fragility   and fortitude

The inevitable conflict
of rank and file
of order and purpose
of hard-boiled birth

It's really about the toast
the butter   the extermination
that leads to bacon
or greasy pan sausage

3.   *Fate*
A chicken crosses the road

the grill of a semi barreling along
Close call   or the splat
of feather and blood

It could go either way

4.   *Farm Fresh*
Every so often, the crack reveals a small clot
trailing from the yolk, a speck that may have been
destined but, instead, congeals in the skillet
glistening with brown butter.

5.   *Free Range*
Once there was a hen whose offspring
were stolen   repeatedly

Once there was a chicken, blind to tire tracks,
just trying to get on with its day.

Georgia Popoff

In Memoriam, for Marian

"Better pass boldly into that other world,
in the full glory of some passion
than fade and wither dismally with age."
James Joyce

One crackling night in midwinter,
some of us gathered around a fireplace
to listen and to read, and to watch the licking flames,
all fired with the full glory of passion.
    Passion for words on pages,
    Passion to hear the words shared,
    to speak some of these words.
    to take turns in the reading.

An odd way to spend an evening, some might say:
grown men and women, reading to each other,
words all had heard before,
stories they already knew.
But in the telling, in the reading,
hearing them open in different ways,
drawing together those who listened.
A new story told.

How do words comprehend a life?
That night, long ago, at a party and reading
about another party,

a party that never happened except in words,
where people were doing just what we were doing:
singing and talking and eating and drinking,
If one of us
should find a way of reading
with insight, a shadow, a word,
flickering, shimmering,
different from what you or I or anyone may have
noticed previously, that thought might travel
outward and circle around.

That's what it means to teach a poem.
That's what theatre is. They are the same.

So, after the passing of one dear friend,
we gathered again near a fire
to read again the same story
made different by her death and our lives.
She had often become the Molly in the story,
who had become the Penelope of myth.

How do women so very different shed light
on each other's lives?
Perhaps that, too, is the magic of words.

Susan Wolstenholme

Susan Murphy, art

Acknowledgements
(In order of appearance)

Let Morning Come first appeared in Heffernan's book *What the Gratitude List Said to the Bucket List*, New York Quarterly Books, The New York Quarterly Foundation, Inc. (2019).

Field Notes: Hand first appeared in Heffernan's book *What the Gratitude List Said to the Bucket List*, New York Quarterly Books, The New York Quarterly Foundation, Inc. (2019).

Recue at Koko Crater first appeared in Heffernan's book *What the Gratitude List Said to the Bucket List*, New York Quarterly Books, The New York Quarterly Foundation, Inc. (2019).

Sailing first appeared in Heffernan's book *What the Gratitude List Said to the Bucket List*, New York Quarterly Books, The New York Quarterly Foundation, Inc. (2019).

Geomorphology, Sharon Souva's quilt art, was accepted in the Quilts Unlimited show in Old Forge, NY.

Wild Woman first appeared in *Boneyard Poetry, A Wild Compilation of Poems.* 2025.

Woman in the Window first appeared in the book *Happy Birthday, Mr. Lincoln,* NLAPW, Pen Women Press, 2009. Note: Rosa Parks died on October 24, 2005. Her brave action on December 1, 1955 became a pivotal, historic moment in the Civil Rights Movement.

Crush on a Dead Guy first appeared in Popoff's book *Living with Haints*, Tiger Bark Press, 2024.

Tea for All the Broken Places first appeared in the *Elizabeth Royal Patton Poetry Prize Anthology 2024*, Clare Songbirds Publishing House.

Summer 1980 first appeared in Popoff's book *Living With Haints*, Tiger Bark Press, 2024.

No Screens in Sight Inspired by J.W. Johnston's art, *"Trailside, 2022."*

Notes in Hollow Spaces read at the Schweinfurth Art Center, in response to Deale Hutton's *Emerald Ash Borer*, 2025. **Notes in Hollow Spaces** first appeared in *An Apple Is Just A Bird With No Beak*, Kelsay Books, 2025.

A few resources from **Catastrophizing is my jam**: *Active Hope: How To Face the Mess We're in without Going Crazy* by Joanna Macy and Chris Johnstone, New World Library, 2012.
Let this Radicalize You: Organizing and The Revolution of Reciprocal Care by Kelly Hayes and Mariame Kaba, Haymarket Books, 2023. Or if you are looking for help coping, check out Paul Shattuck's Substack, *Progressive Strategy Now.*

Reflections previously appeared online as a *Featured Poem* on the NLAPW.org website.

Untact first appeared in the journal *Plainsongs*, Summer 2022, Corpus Callosum Press.

Opening Day of Hunting Season first appeared in Clark's book *Watershed, new Finger Lake Poems* (Kelsay Books, 2023).

Planet Earth Hanging first published in *The Healing Muse* 2026, Upstate Medical University, Syracuse, NY, under a different title: "Immigration…Policy…Pause."

The Gentle Arts first appeared in *The Loneliest Places* (Three Hills Press, 2022).

Ovum Suite first appeared in Popoff's book *Living With Haints*, Tiger Bark Press, 2024.

Joan Applebaum, art

CNY Branch Pen Women Contributors

(A) Joan Applebaum is a visual artist who has exhibited in juried competitions throughout Northern NY and Coastal Delaware. Her paintings of the regions are in private collections across the US and abroad. She holds memberships in the CNY and Holly Branches of the NLAPW. To see her work, visit www.windyhillstudioarts.com.

(L) Nancy Keats Benson is a retired Speech-Language Pathologist. She has several poetry books and a children's mystery book published. She's had numerous poems published in magazines and anthologies. Recently she had a nature poem published in an anthology, *Love Letters to Gaia*.

(A) Linda Bigness holds a BFA from Syracuse University and a MA in art history from SUNY Empire. Her work has been collected and exhibited throughout the United States. Her paintings hang in private collections, galleries and in the Rochester New York Regional Health Center.

(A)(L) Sheila M. Byrnes is a genealogist, freelance writer, and mixed-media artist. She has been published in several national magazines and formerly wrote the *CNYGS E-News*, a national bi-weekly genealogy newsletter. Byrnes serves as the NLAPW National President and as the National Historian.

(L) Carolyn Clark is a poet with a PhD in Classics whose works include *Watershed* – new Finger Lakes poems, *Poet Duet: A Mother and Daughter, Choose Lethe, New Found Land, Mnemosyne: the Long Traverse*. A writing coach and editor, she currently enjoys creating "made-for- you" poems (QWERTY) at Ithaca Farmers Market.

(L) Nancy Avery Dafoe writes across genres and has fifteen books. A memoir about her son, *Unstuck in Time,* won the Director's Choice in Indie Book Awards for Humam Relations, among other national awards. She serves as the NLAPW Second Vice President.

(L) Janine M. DeBaise is the author of two collections of poetry, *Body Language* and *Of a Feather*. Her essays have appeared in *Orion, Southwest Review*, and *Prairie Schooner*, amongst others. She won the Vinnie Ream Medal for her essay *The Space Between*. Her book *Sky Gone Weird: Change, Loss, and Other Perks of Nature* will be published in 2026.

(L) Rachel Dickinson holds an MFA in Nonfiction. Author of seven nonfiction books including *Falconer on the Edge* (Houghton Mifflin Harcourt) and *The Loneliest Places* (Cornell Press), she's also written for many publications including, *The Atlantic, Audubon*, and *The Saturday Evening Post*. She was a NYS Rural & Traditional Arts Fellow, 2024.

(A) Karen E. Dillon is a photographer, poet, and painter. Her muse is nature, especially the moods of water. She was a wood-working artisan before returning to her early love of photography, then to painting. She has won awards in both photography and watercolor, exhibits in local art shows, and practices "plein air" painting, selling to private collectors.

(L) Janet Clare Fagal is a retired teacher and poet. Janet's poems have won Pen Women Biennial contests. Her poems appear in *The Pen Woman*, at NLAPW.org and in anthologies for children and adults including in *I am Someone Else*, compiled by Lee Bennett Hopkins.

(A) Marilyn Forth had a distinguished art and teaching career, serving as Professor in Textile Art at Syracuse University, and with the American Craft Council, NYC. She has shown her work around the country, as well as at the Edgewood Gallery and other locations in Syracuse.

(L) Mary L. Gardner's poems have appeared in fourteen anthologies, including NLAPW, Syracuse Poster Project, Upstate Medical University. FootHills Publishing has published her three chapbooks of poetry. She holds a Master in Public Health from Johns Hopkins University and a Certificate in Poetry from the Syracuse DWC.

(L) Lisa Harris is an award-winning writer and educator. Her novels *Geechee Girls, Alleghany Dream*, and *The Raven's Tale for The Quest Trilogy* have been categorized as Northern Appalachian literature. Her poetry chapbooks are *Broken Open, Dwelling Space, Awash in Color*, and *Traveling through Glass*.

(L) Gloria Heffernan's fifth book, *Twilight Garden,* will be published in 2026. Her previous books are *Fused* (Shanti Arts Books), *Exploring Poetry of Presence* (Back Porch Productions), *Peregrination: Poems for Antarctica* (Kelsay Books), and *What the Gratitude List Said to the Bucket List,* (NYQ Books).

(L) Karen Foresti Hempson is a retired professor of Social Studies education. Her essays "Synchronicity" and "Humiliation" were published in *Stone Canoe* and *28 Voices*. She currently serves as Branch Secretary. Her creative non-fiction book, *Bean Pickers*, was published in 2019. Her YA historical fiction *Shellback* was published in the Fall 2024.

(A)(L) Vanessa Johnson is a Griot, writer, playwright, actor, fiber artist, and teaching artist telling tales of Africa, and Social Justice. Johnson's band *"Matie Masie"* transforms works into performances. Her program *"Griot Guides"* taught storytelling. She has served as the program director for the Matilda Joslyn Gage Ambassadors for Human Rights.

(L) Gretchen Martens is a writer and editor who lived in Pennsylvania and has since moved to Texas but has chosen to join our CNY Branch. She operates the Scholar's Couch editing service and The Village of Care Press. Her books include *Untying the Yellow Ribbon: Transforming How Veterans and Communities Thrive.*

(L) Nicole Marie Mastropool has a background in Criminal Justice, Psychology, and Criminology. Her interest in true crime and horror is evident in her darker-themed works. Pursuing careers in criminal justice and teaching, Nicole's commitment to writing never wavered. She has published poetry, children's books, and an anthology.

(L) Stacey Murphy is a poet who enjoys finding connections with human experience in nature around the Finger Lakes, has a heart-shaped rock obsession. Her first poetry collection, *Old Stones Understand* (Shanti Arts, 2021) won a Royal Dragonfly Award. She co-edited *NY Votes for Women: A Suffrage Centennial Anthology* (Cayuga Lake Books, 2017), fostering her love of encouraging writers.

(A) Susan W. Murphy is an award-winning visual artist, who has been showing her work for almost 50 years in regional, national, and international shows. She recently won awards in the 2024 Philadelphia Water Color Society's International Works on Paper and the Cooperstown 2025 National Exhibition. You can find her work at swmurphy2020.

(L) Carolyn Ostrander, a managing editor for *The Comstock Review*, is a poet, scholar and advocate for rural schools, disability rights, and public history. Some recent poems have appeared in *Beyond Words, Last Stanza Poetry Journal, Amethyst Review*, and *The Comstock Review,* with articles in *Stone Canoe, Good Day Magazine, Reclaiming the Rural,* and *Oralité et Gestualité.*

(L) Bobbie Dumas Panek has published *Morning Walks: Zen Meditations*; *An Apple Is Just a Bird with a Beak*, and *Just Another Day*. Her poems appeared in aaduna.org, and moondance.org, *The Pen Woman* (NLAPW), and in other anthologies. Her articles have appeared in *Birds and Blooms, Reminisce Extra,* and literary magazines. She is a former editor of *The Pen Woman.*

(L) Kimberly Parr is a civil servant by day, crime writer by night. After a career penning award-winning ads and feature articles for publications ranging from *Equine Journal* to *Roofing Magazine*, Kimberly now writes about unsolved crimes. She also has a fascination with the Erie Canal, an engineering marvel awash in weirdness. Visit her at IceColdCases.com.

(L) Georgia A. Popoff, teaches for the YMCA of Central NY's Writers Voice and serves as Poet Laureate of Onondaga County, NY (2022-2025). Her fifth collection is *Living with Haints* (Tiger Bark Press, 2024). She is the editor for the University of Michigan Press *Under Discussion* book series on contemporary poets.

(A) Mary Raineri is a textural artist whose abstract work straddles two and three-dimensional form. She integrates a wide variety of mixed media, including wood and fiber, metal and stone, acrylics, encaustics, inks and oils which are combined in collages and assemblages.

(L) Railey Jane Savage lives in central New York. With an English degree from Smith College, she is a writer and editor. She has two published books: *A Century of Swindles: Ponzi Schemes, Con Men, and Fraudsters*, (2021, Rowman & Littlefield); and *We Have a Winner; America's Weird and Wonderful Races, Derbies, Pageants, and Eating Contests* (2017, Lyons Press).

(A) Sharon Souva is a fabric artist whose art has hung in many shows in upstate New York. She teaches color theory and drawing classes at Onondaga Community College. She lives in Syracuse, NY. You can see her beautiful artwork at www.SharonBottleSouva.com.

(A) Joan Stier is who has made a living for many years creating artwork. Her medium is primarily watercolor/ink painting on various subjects from the realistic to the abstract. She has won numerous awards, and her work may be found in the collections of thousands of owners around the country.

(A) Sally Stormon is an artist. She made her living for many years as a mental health counselor. She tries to capture light with her watercolor paintings and often exhibits in the National Exhibition of American Watercolors, The Art of New York, and other national exhibitions.

(L) Priscilla Berggren-Thomas is a retired librarian and a full-time dog lover. She has written articles on feminism and spirituality and written a column for *The Cortland Standard* called *Raised by Wolves* for over ten years. She also dabbles in writing fantasy.

(L) Laura Thorne is the CEO at Wildebeest Publishing Company. She is an entrepreneur with a background in environmental science, writing, and coaching. She is a certified project management professional, helping to ensure all projects run smoothly. She has traveled the world.

(L) Susan Wolstenholme is professor emerita at Cayuga Community College, where she worked for 45 years. She is the author of Gothic (Re)visions): Writing Women as Readers (SUNY Press) and editor of the Oxford University Press World's Classics edition of The *Wonderful Wizard of Oz*, and has appeared in several theatrical productions.

*(A) represents Artist members belonging to the NLAPW.

*(L) represents Letters members or writers belonging to the NLAPW.